She could see everything.

Adam's clothes made a messy trail across the floor; the tub was filled to the brim, the water perfectly clear. Five feet ten inches of presumably naked man was sunk into it up to his armpits.

With his eyes closed.

Loath to disturb him, but drawn inside nonetheless, Julia inched closer. Adam didn't move so much as an eyelash. She should wake him up, she thought, before his bones boiled down to jelly. *Soon as she got a good long look.*

The thought of all that exposed skin—wet, warm and male—made her fingers twitch. What would happen if she touched him? Very, very lightly?

She leaned over the tub, one hand extended, one finger unfurling…

'What are you looking for?' His eyes were open. Electric. She sprang back, but his fingers were already locked around her wrist. She didn't try to escape. Why run when all she really wanted was to stay?

His quiet question hung in the air. *What are you looking for?*

'You,' she said. *For the past ten years.*

Dear Reader,

When I began writing *Smooth Moves* (Sensual Romance™ SR91, May 2002), I wasn't thinking of doing a spin-off book. But as I developed Zack Brody's story his somewhat mysterious brother Adam became a large part of the plot, even though he remained offstage. Then Julia Knox popped up, hinting at her history with Adam—what did happen on the night of her eighteenth birthday?—and I knew there was another story to be told.

So here we go again! Zack and Cathy are getting married. The admiral's on hand, along with the Heartbroken, and you'll get to read more about the Brody family, too. Would I forget Lauren? She deserves a 'special' hero of her very own…though some might call him her comeuppance.

Welcome back to Quimby!

Carrie

PS I love to hear from readers. Please write to me by clicking on my name in the author pages at www.eHarlequin.com.

RISKY MOVES

by

Carrie Alexander

MILLS & BOON®

All the characters in this book have no existence outside the imagination of the author, and have no relation whatsoever to anyone bearing the same name or names. They are not even distantly inspired by any individual known or unknown to the author, and all the incidents are pure invention.

First published in Great Britain 2003
by Harlequin Mills & Boon Limited,
Eton House, 18-24 Paradise Road, Richmond, Surrey TW9 1SR

ISBN 0 263 83542 1

21-0203

Printed and bound in Spain
by Litografia Rosés S.A., Barcelona

Prologue

*"*THIS IS THE BEST IDEA *you've ever had," Julia said, trying to convince herself. She sat on the edge of the bed, careful not to muss the spread, and folded her hands in her lap. "Quit fussing. Just sit and wait. He'll be here any minute."*

A bottle of the most expensive champagne she could afford—fifteen dollars—was chilling in the motel's plastic ice bucket. Red roses were positioned on the mirrored bureau so that the reflection made the bouquet seem doubly extravagant. She'd brought along every candle she could scrounge up and had placed them all around the room, giving the anonymous space a romantic glow. She'd even bought a box of condoms and put on the sexiest lingerie she owned—a peach silk robe and matching slip-style nightie.

The minutes ticked by. Julia tightened her threaded fingers. When her stomach fluttered, she told herself it was nerves, not misgivings.

The stage was set. She knew what she was doing.

Complete physical intimacy was the next step in a logical progression.

It was time for her to make love with Zack Brody.

1

Ten years later

EVEN AT THE BEST of times, Adam Brody didn't care for wedding receptions. The clamoring crowd, the overabundant feast, the cloying scents of flowers, perfume and aftershave—not his style. But it was clear that rock-bottom bad had been achieved when the maid of honor walked up to him and said, "I want to defy death."

The wedding had gone off without a hitch. And, really, Adam had nothing to complain about, considering that he'd tolerated far worse ordeals. Like three months in a hospital bed flat on his back. He'd been managing—aside from his stint as toastmaster general—to fly below the radar of most of the guests.

That is, until Julia Knox made her big pronouncement.

Adam nearly swallowed the toothpick from the little sugared grape and melting cheese thingamabob he'd just popped into his mouth. The Quimby Woodwind Trio was playing a reedy rendition of "Sunrise, Sunset," which meant his slow torture was almost over. He was one round of goodbyes away from freedom.

First he'd have to deal with Julia. Of all the words he'd imagined she might say when they met again, "I want to defy death" weren't among them.

Carefully he removed the frilled toothpick from his mouth. "Pardon?"

"I want to defy death." She looked straight at him with serious hazel eyes. Julia was almost always serious. Which was why he couldn't fathom—

"Teach me how," she said. Forcefully. Without blinking. As if she weren't wearing several hundred dollars worth of tulle and a floral headpiece that made her look like Heidi of the Alps.

Weddings did strange things to women's heads, inside and out. After Adam's one brush with the phenomenon had ended in catastrophe across the board, he'd renewed his policy to avoid contact with marriage-minded females whenever possible. The fact that his older brother, Zack, was today's groom and that he'd played the best man had necessitated some pretty fancy footwork—especially for a gimp. Luckily Zack understood, having endured three solid months of his fiancée's obsession with color matching, ribbon tying and invitation lists.

Plain and simple, weddings made women nuts.

Julia Knox, however...

She wasn't the type.

Maybe she'd changed in the years since Adam had left Quimby, his small Midwestern hometown. Calm, reasonable Julia was the woman least likely to change, but, hey—anything was possible.

Adam tilted his head. In spite of his vow to stay detached, she'd aroused his curiosity.

"This might not be the ideal time to bring this up," she said, "but it's now or never. For such a prominent member of the wedding party, you've been rather elusive."

He shrugged, remaining silent. She had to know why.

Her brows shot up. "I suppose you've been thrust under the Quimby microscope whenever you show your face?"

"It's not my face they're interested in."

Not one for sidelong looks and whispers behind hands, Julia ran her gaze over his tuxedo-clad body, from the tightly knotted bow tie to the black satin cummerbund and all the way down to the rented patent leather wing tips that pinched his toes. She lingered openly over his troublesome legs. A majority of the wedding guests had done the same, particularly when he'd offered his arm to escort Julia down the aisle. He'd wondered if they were waiting for him to stumble.

Julia's interest was concerned and kind, not speculative. Although his reaction—a hot flush of awareness—was disconcerting, he put it down to more of the same. Ergo, further humiliation. His aversion to being the object of curiosity and gossip was a large part of his dislike for the otherwise acceptable reception. He'd joined the wedding party at the last moment and had planned to duck out of the reception as soon as possible, until his sense of obligation had stopped him. He could be elusive. He couldn't be rude, not at Zack's wedding. He owed his brother his life.

Involuntarily, Adam shifted from foot to foot as the muscles in his lower back and left hip started to quiver and contract. *It's only tension,* he thought, concentrating on relaxing the tightness before it became a spasm. He imagined a clear, cold river washing over him. Through him.

Relax. It's only Julia.

Her forthright gaze returned to his face. She didn't say anything about how "good, really good" he looked. She only blinked, let go of her concern and then reassumed the determined set of her mouth. No pity from Julia, he thought. *Thanks, Goldie.*

She took a breath. "You wouldn't know it to look at me—" when she touched the beaded bodice of her wedding getup he obligingly looked at the *me* part of her that swelled in the scooped neckline "—but my life is dull. I need a few thrills and chills. A challenge to shake up the status quo. I figure you're the guy to come to." She gestured with one hand. A delicate pearl bracelet slid over her smooth forearm. His gaze shifted, catching on it, then on the fragile knob of her wrist bone, and just like that he couldn't look away. He didn't know why, except that suddenly there was a swirling in his gut, like a strong, sucking whirlpool.

"I need to take a few risks. Feel the rush." She hesitated, putting her hands on her hips, her face infused with the drama of it all. "Teach me how to be a daredevil, Adam."

Oh, no, he thought at once.

Not him. Not her. After all these years, definitely not her.

His silence would have been leaden if not for the clarinets. The song ended on a long, wobbly note, and he shrugged negligently, as if he really didn't care about any of it. "Go eat a chunk of wedding cake, Goldie. The sugar high will cure you." He turned away, trying to pretend he hadn't seen the hurt that had lightning-flashed over her face.

She grasped his sleeve. "Just like old times, is it? You cuffing me on the shoulder and then running away? I know a brush-off when I get one, Adam Brody."

"I'm not sure that you do."

She looked at his sleeve. Deliberately unclenched her fingers as she said in a low voice, "No one calls me Goldie these days."

"Too high school now that you're a mature adult and upstanding citizen?"

She made a face at herself. "Seems like I've always been a mature adult, doesn't it?"

No, he thought, remembering with a startling clarity the one time she'd been as reckless as he, Quimby's notorious daredevil. It wasn't something they talked about. For the past ten years, they'd been very good at avoiding the slightest mention of it. To Adam, Julia Knox was his brother's girlfriend and she always would be. End of story.

"Zack is married," she said, reading his face. "It's official. Lock, stock and honeymoon."

"That doesn't change our—" Adam stopped. Or did it? With marriage, was the unspoken law that brothers don't share the same girl no longer in effect? For a moment, he experienced a glorious relief. His longtime burden of guilt shifted—a boulder rocking at the first wedge of the crowbar. Then he thought of Laurel Barnard, who'd caused a rift between them so immense only a near tragedy had closed it, and the boulder rolled firmly back into place.

"It's been years since Zack and I broke up." Julia produced a rusty chuckle. "I think you and I are allowed to be...friends." Her lashes lowered. He saw her swallow.

Nervous? he wondered. *Unsure? Julia?*

"Sure." He nodded, acting agreeable only to get out of the tight spot. He had no intention of taking up with her—she was far too dangerous to his status quo. "No problem. We've always been friends, right?" He gave her arm a strictly friendly squeeze, and there went the whirlpool again. They weren't friends, he reminded himself, stepping away from the buffet tables. They couldn't be.

Because they shared a secret. And it was a whopper. Too gigantic and shameful to openly discuss. But it would always be there, looming between them, as unscalable as a sheer rock wall.

"Then there's no reason you can't teach me how to sky dive," Julia said in a flurry, aware that he was desperate to get away.

That stopped him. He cocked his head again. "Sky dive? You've got to be kidding."

"I'm serious. It's the riskiest thing I can think of."

"You're nuts." Flat-out nuts. And he was no longer sure it was the wedding that had gotten to her. She seemed rational enough about Zack's marriage, what with being the maid of honor and all, so maybe that wasn't what was freaking her out.

Still...

Julia Knox—skydiving? Conventional Julia, the pretty, popular, nice girl who'd been nicknamed Goldie after Fort Knox, although privately he'd always considered the name a suitable tribute to her shining example of female perfection. Zack Brody and Julia Knox had been the perfect Ken-and-Barbie couple of Quimby High School—basketball captain and head cheerleader, class president and Honor Society inductee, homecoming king and queen. They went together like sugar and cream.

A few years, a little trauma—even Zack's marriage to Cathy Timmerman—couldn't change the essence of that. Julia Knox didn't need to shake up her life. She was, and always would be, twenty-four-karat gold.

"You've been watching 'Road Rules' again," he scoffed. "Or maybe travel documentaries on the adventure channel?"

"Don't condescend, Adam."

He smiled at her stubborn resolve. Maybe her sweet nature had turned a little tart in the years he'd been away. "Sorry. It's just that you of all people—" He looked her up and down. "Out of everyone I know, you're the person with her feet most firmly stuck to the ground."

"Exactly the point."

He shook his head. "Don't ask me to help you with this crazy idea. Go to a skydiving school if you have to, but don't ask me."

She reached for his hands and almost got them, too, except that he backed off. He was still quick enough for an elusive maneuver when he needed one. Too bad that meant he was trapped in the far corner of Jerome's, blocked from the exit by a jumbled maze of guests, fancy-dressed tables and chairs at cockeyed angles. The john was nearby, but what he really needed was to get outside and breathe the fresh night air.

"Adam," Julia said, her voice catching. He quit scanning the room for an escape route and focused on her face, intrigued despite himself. What was going on in her unleveled head? "I guess I'm scared," she confessed. Her eyes beseeched him, shimmering with a surprising amount of emotion. "That's why I asked you. I want someone I know I can trust. Not a stranger."

"Moot point. I'm not certified to teach skydiving in this state."

"Oh." She frowned, stymied for a moment before her troubled brow smoothed. "Rock climbing, then. To begin."

He could do that. Take her out to one of the granite bluffs he'd scrambled up and down as a kid, make her think it was steep and dangerous, give her enough of a thrill to satisfy whatever urge was driving her and pack it in before lunchtime. He could do that. Maybe.

Maybe.

Doubt crept in. He hated it. He'd never been cautious or afraid before the accident—hiking, biking, rowing, parachuting and rappelling without a moment's fear. Even now, eighteen months after the accident, when he'd recovered to the point where walking was again a given instead of a small miracle...it wasn't enough. He was supposed to feel blessed, and instead he was so damned uneasy about his abilities. Not to mention his future.

Julia blinked, growing dismayed by his hesitation. "Oh, Adam. I'm sor—" She stopped herself, her features crimping with concern as her gaze swept over his legs. "I thought—Zack said you're doing great—"

"No problem." Adam was brisk about it, though suddenly he was having trouble swallowing. His fingers felt like thumbs as he yanked at the bow tie until it finally came undone. Julia didn't need to know how feeble he'd been, what a long struggle it had taken to regain even half of the physical skills he'd lost when he'd sped too fast around a treacherous curve on a mountain road and sideswiped a lumbering delivery van. After surviving a succession of risky adventures, he'd been done in by a squat van transporting inner tubes for the Snake River Rafters. The irony wasn't as amusing as it might have been.

"It's you I'm concerned with," he said bluntly. "You've never been the daring type. What's up?"

Julia met his eyes, her chin dimpled like an orange peel because her lips were so firmly set. He held back the impulse to smile. Being deadly serious, she wouldn't appreciate knowing how cute she looked. "You think I can't handle it?" she accused. "I'm fit, you know. I work out." She lifted an arm, crooking her elbow and clenching a fist to show him her biceps. "I'm perfectly capable and—and mentally prepared."

"To defy death?"

"Um. That might have been an overstatement."

To get his attention—which she had. But he still had no idea of her reasoning. "All this because you're bored?"

Her eyes narrowed. "Why do you do it?"

His tight answering smile was an evasion. "I don't remember." Didn't want to remember was more like it. Remembering would mean wanting, and wanting meant trying. There were times, he'd learned, that it hurt too much to try. Which was something he'd never expected to cop to, considering all the do-or-die instances when he'd hung off a rock wall with his muscles screaming, forcing his numb fingertips to clench on a handhold just...one...more...time.

"I remember," Julia said. Her face softened. "You've been a daredevil ever since Chuck Cheswick double-dog dared you to climb the water tower when you were ten. I also remember how you used to scare the life out of Zack. He was always watching over your escapades."

"And bailing me out."

"Yes, and bailing you out." It was obvious what they were both thinking of now. About a year and a half ago, there'd been a blowup between him and Zack over Laurel Barnard, the woman Adam had fallen for in a bad way. Laurel had manipulated the situation, playing one brother against the other until they were twisted into knots. After a major argument, Adam had made a heated escape, leaving Laurel to worm out of Zack what she'd been after all along—a marriage proposal from the man known as Heartbreak Brody, the biggest catch in Quimby. A short time later, Adam's car accident had called Zack to Idaho on the eve of the wedding—trumping Laurel's worst-laid plans.

Adam figured he owed Zack double. First for saving him from the scheming Laurel, then for saving him from despair when the doctors had told him he might not walk again. Zack had stayed for an entire year, putting his life and reputation on hold to inspire, cajole and harangue Adam until he was back on his feet. Performing as the best man at his brother's *real* wedding despite the curious stares and pitying attention was the least Adam could do in return.

"Hey, Madman," said Fred Spangler, waving from a group of plotting groomsmen. "Get over here, fella. We've gotta strategize over how to trash the groom's getaway car."

Adam looked at Julia. "Sorry. Duty calls."

"But what about—"

He stepped around her when she didn't move. "Nice talking to you."

She reached out for a brief, firm hug, sending a jolt through him. Usually she kept her distance. "It's wonderful to see you again," she murmured. "You look..."

Good. Really good! Adam gritted his teeth in anticipation.

Julia swung her head, making her smooth golden-brown hair sweep across the small satin bows that lay flat against her shoulders. "You look thoroughly civilized."

Civilized?

"Hey—what does that mean?" Adam said, but Fred Spangler grabbed his arm and pulled him away, leaving Julia looking after him with a taunting little smile playing across her lips.

THE WOODWIND TRIO played a slow, spitty-sounding Irish melody to wind down the evening as Julia made her way across the restaurant to her table. A slice of wedding cake waited at her place, thickly frosted with green and white globs that were supposed to be lily of the valley even though this was an autumn wedding. Julia had advised Cathy that detailed artistry was beyond Velda Thompson, Quimby's one and only unrenowned cake decorator, but you couldn't talk sense to a woman about to tie the knot. Brides had their own cockeyed logic. A mystery to Julia, who liked order, stability, cause and effect. Under normal circumstances, she couldn't imagine thinking like a bride.

But these circumstances weren't normal.

Her tablemates were off chatting, boozing or schmoozing, so Julia allowed herself a loud sigh, then propped her elbows on the table. Disconsolate, she considered the cake a long while before stabbing it with a fork. There was no need to sleep with a slice of wedding cake under her pillow. She didn't want marriage just now—she wanted change. Excitement.

Adam Brody.

The sooner the better.

Ever since Cathy had confided that Adam had agreed to return to Quimby and act as Zack's best man, Julia had been filled with an unusual restless energy. This was her last chance to follow the road not taken. She was certain.

Either she put the vitality back into her life or she settled for more of the same. Either she made Adam see her in a new light or she gave him up for good. A woman could live modestly and pine after a man for only so long before she became pathetic.

For these many years, she'd been careful to keep her feelings for Adam Brody secret. But some of her friends must suspect by now. Cathy knew, for certain, which meant Zack probably did. Being Zack, as honorable as he was handsome, he'd been completely discreet about the potential complications. Julia had no doubt that he'd offer his blessing, if it ever came to that.

Ever?

Or never?

Julia shivered. She could face never if she had to. There were worse things.

Like skydiving.

Oh, good grief, what was she thinking? Adam was right. She wasn't the type. Just as she wasn't *his* type.

Redheaded Allie Spangler came over and plopped into a chair. She eyed the wedding cake, pierced by an upright fork. "Aren't you going to eat that?" she asked hungrily. Her gaze darted around the elegant restaurant, searching for Fred. She and her husband had been on a diet for several months now, but she was always sneaking snacks behind his back.

Julia nudged the plate toward her longtime friend. "Feel free."

"Adam's looking really good." Allie moaned as she scooped a dollop of sugary frosting on her fingertip. "I halfway expected a wasted shell of a man, but..." She glanced at the gaggle of groomsmen, smacking her lips. "He hardly even limps."

"Yes." Julia didn't need to follow Allie's stare. An image of Adam was burned on her mind. His tousled brown hair, the lean, athletic body in a rumpled tux, tie undone, collar open. His face. His sober face. Always intense, but now hardened by an intimate knowledge of struggle and pain. And so...guarded. It hurt her to look at him, knowing what he'd been through. Except when the boyish daredevil grin emerged, even briefly, reminding her of the mischievous kid he'd been, the cocky athlete he'd become. Under the austere exterior, he was still the restless young man she'd fallen for more than ten years ago—fallen for as fast and hard as a sky diver with a malfunctioning parachute.

"Aw. Don't look so mournful."

Julia shot a curious look at Allie, who smiled through a mouthful of cake.

"Just because Heartbreak is off the market for good..." The redhead spoke soothingly.

"Oh. Yes, of course. Heartbreak." Julia smiled, mimicking the brave faces of the single women in attendance. Zack "Heartbreak" Brody had been the most eligible bachelor in Quimby. Some of his ex-girlfriends had formed an informal support group, calling themselves the Heartbroken, sisters in misery. Along with Allie, Julia had been a founding member, even though her feelings for Zack were not nearly as significant as the others suspected.

Not for *Zack.*

"I'm fine with that," she said, ever so brightly.

Allie patted her hand. "Sure you are."

"Zack and Cathy are perfect together. I'm thrilled for them."

"Yeah, yeah. We all are." Allie's smile wound tighter and tighter until her homely freckled face was all squinched up, twisting her expression into a grimace. She released it, casting a guilty glance at Fred. "Anyhoo. A bunch of us are getting together after to commiserate—er, to celebrate. Har, har."

Julia murmured something noncommittal. She wasn't in the mood to listen to Allie and Gwen and the Thompson twins and other assorted singletons moan and groan about their great unrequited love for Zack.

When it came to the Brody men, she knew too well how they felt. And it didn't pay to linger on it.

Action, she reminded herself. She'd promised that this time she would go into action instead of sitting and waiting for Adam to come to her. No more doing the right thing. No more boring, well-behaved good girl.

"It's a warm night for October. We were talking about a bonfire on the beach, just like old times. Some of the guys are coming, too." Allie chuckled. "With liquor, I betcha. They're thinking if they get a few of you bridesmaids comfortably numb, the pickings will be easy."

Julia started to shake her head, then stopped. "Will—um, who's going?"

"Me and Fred. Gwen, Karen and Kelly. I don't know about Faith—she's been even quieter than usual lately. Probably grieving over Zack. All of the groomsmen will be there, and maybe one or two of the guys from Fred and Zack's basketball league."

"Adam?" Julia blurted.

Allie polished off the cake before she answered. "It was his idea. You know Adam."

Never indoors when he could be out. Always the first to move, to dare, to go. Farther and farther away each time, harder and harder to catch up to.

He was a comet, burning through the sky. She was only Julia Knox, her feet stuck on the ground. If she reached for him, she might be badly burned. Did she dare try?

I have to. This is my last chance.

"I'll be there," she said. "After I go home and change."

Allie scanned the pumpkin-colored dress. It was too frou-frou for Julia's taste, but out of solidarity with her fellow Quimby shopkeepers, Cathy had insisted on patronizing the lone local bridal shop—where tasteful choices were woefully limited. The dresses at Bridal Bonanza got a lot worse than frou-frou.

"Always a bridesmaid, huh?" Allie said with a bit of an edge, because she hadn't been asked to be one. Although outwardly happy in her marriage, her interference in Zack's love life had once gone too far. Fortunately for her, Zack and Cathy were forgiving sorts.

Julia smiled too sweetly. "Maybe we can *all* move on now that Zack's off the market for good."

Allie shrugged, quickly changing subjects. "There's always Adam, I guess. Even if he's not much of a marriage prospect. No steady job, no house, no savings account..."

I already have those things, Julia thought. *Turns out they're not enough.*

"...and now there are his weak legs and all. He's sure not the kind of guy you can count on."

Julia disagreed. She knew firsthand that though Adam wasn't as perfect as his brother—he made mistakes, and she'd been one of them—he also had enough pride, courage and loyalty for ten men. In many ways, however, even though they were the same age and had grown up in the same small town and attended the same school, he was still an enigma to her. He was so disciplined, yet utterly reckless, seemingly fearless. She'd always found him fascinating, the kind of man who would challenge her to be more than expected.

And she needed such a challenge. She needed it *now.*

Julia forced herself to focus on the conversation instead of her secret desires. "You know Adam better than me," she told Allie with a shrug, even though that wasn't completely true. Allie, who'd lived next door to the Brody brothers, had been buddies—only buddies—with both of them. She and Adam had egged each other on in their pranks and misadventures, with Zack the guardian who was always there to get them out of trouble.

"Sure, but I never woulda dated him." Allie was watching the men, who apparently thought they were slipping out of the restaurant unnoticed. Fred Spangler tiptoed past the bar, as if a two-hundred-pound car salesman with a mop of curly blond hair could sneak anywhere. His wife shook her head fondly. "I like a beefier man." She chuckled. "And I got me a steer."

"I didn't date him, either," Julia said, her eyes on Adam. He moved easily between the tables, avoiding hails of recognition by keeping his gaze focused on the exit.

Eyes on the exit. That was Adam Brody to a T.

"Nope." Allie had switched her attention to the newlyweds. "It was always you and Zack, two peas in a pod."

Adam looked over his shoulder at the last moment, straight at Julia. A telling warmth bloomed in her cheeks. She'd been wanting him for too many years to be able to switch her feelings off fast enough to completely hide them from his notice. Not even years of practice made perfect.

She swallowed past the lump forming in her throat. "Maybe we were too perfect together," she heard herself saying, as if from a distance. All her energy was focused on Adam, who broke their moment of mutual awareness as quickly as he'd started it. He slipped beyond her sight, the heavy carved doors of the former bank building closing solidly behind him.

"How's that?" Allie asked.

Julia waved a vague hand, waiting for her hammering pulse to fade. "Um, you know. There was no lasting heat." Not a problem as far as Adam was concerned, even with very little encouragement.

Zack had been her first love, a puppy love, the summer she was sixteen. Adam hadn't caught her attention in that way then—he was still a scrawny boy, always off poking around in the woods and climbing anything vertical, including the post office flagpole. Zack had been slightly older, a handsome icon of maturity and popularity, working as the lifeguard at the Mirror Lake beach. Everyone had said they belonged together. Soon Julia and Zack believed it, too. And since they were the kind of people who did what was expected of them, they'd lasted longer than they ought to have.

"No heat?" Allie repeated. "C'mon. I remember how you two always looked so right together. High-school sweethearts. Every girl in town envied you."

"That was years ago. We broke up, remember?"

Allie reached for a beribboned party-favor bag and tore apart the netting with her fingernails. Pastel mints and candied almonds spilled across the tablecloth. She began popping them in her mouth one by one until her lips were puckered. "And it's just coincidence that you haven't been serious with anyone since?"

"I've dated," Julia said. "Plenty." At least by Quimby standards.

"Yeah, stodgy guys with briefcases and beepers."

"Suits me fine. I have my own briefcase and beeper." Julia nibbled an almond. After working for one of the nationwide real-estate franchises for a few years, she'd come back to Quimby to open her own agency. It was doing very well, by Quimby standards.

"Which is why you need the opposite, of course!" Cathy Timmerman—Cathy Brody, Julia remembered—swooped on them with the numerous layers of her swagged ivory skirts bunched in her hands. She kicked out a chair with the toe of a dyed-to-match ivory pump and collapsed with a loud exhale. "Gad. Weddings really take it out of you."

"But the honeymoon puts it back in," Julia said, giving Cathy's hand a squeeze. Quite a reach over their voluminous, rustling gowns.

"No, that's the groom's job," Allie said mischievously.

Cathy groaned. "Please, no more bawdy honeymoon jokes. I've had enough of those from Zack's uncle Brady. Brady Brody, if you can believe it. That's him in the magenta velvet tux. He thinks it's funny to sneak into every picture our photographer takes."

"I remember Uncle Brady," Julia said. "He used to pinch my derriere at family functions. Consider yourself forewarned, Cath."

"Too late. He got in a good one right there in the receiving line. But with all these layers of tulle and genuine polyester silk, what was the point?"

They laughed.

"Zack didn't tell me about his relatives," Cathy continued. "Turns out there are heaps of them." She tried to frown, but nothing could take away the happiness that wreathed her face as clearly as the floral headpiece framed her sable hair. Despite the over-the-top Bridal Bonanza finery, Julia had never seen a bride who glowed more than Cathy. There was no doubt that Zack had chosen right this time around.

"We booked hotel rooms all over the county, and it still seems as though most of them are bunking in at either Zack's house or mine. We haven't managed a moment to ourselves for days and days."

Then neither would Adam, Julia thought, knowing how much he'd hate that.

"When do you escape?" Allie asked, crunching.

"Very soon now." Cathy's eyes gleamed with anticipation as they followed Zack, who was making one last turn around the room, distributing thanks and handshakes. "I can hardly wait." She looked sidelong at her grinning friends. "Not for *that*. For the peace and quiet." She paused, reflecting. "And maybe some of that, too."

Cathy was a lucky bride, Julia told herself. Her groom was an exceptional man. Julia had known so even before a dozen Quimby busybodies had taken it upon themselves to inform her that she'd let a good one get away. She had no hope of explaining why their chemistry hadn't worked when she didn't understand it herself. Put Zack together with Cathy, a relative newcomer to Quimby, and the pair of them smoked. You could practically see the steam rising from their pores.

Maybe it was the comfort and normalcy that had

doomed Julia's relationship with Zack. And that continued to doom her with the few acceptable men she'd encountered since. Briefcases, beepers and boredom—she knew them far too well.

The other two women were discussing the honeymoon plans, six days of autumnal marital bliss at a mountain resort. "By the time we return, I'm hoping all the relatives will have gone," Cathy confessed in a whisper. "It's going to be cozy enough as it is, living right next door to Zack's parents until our new house is built."

"And Adam, too," Julia said. "If he stays, that is."

"Oh, his mother's working on that. Whereas Zack said we were lucky that his brother agreed to fly in last night instead of putting it off until this morning. I hear Adam's always been impossible to peg down."

"He missed the rehearsal dinner." Julia had been all pins and needles, anticipating the sight of him. Instead her first glimpse had come this afternoon, in the church itself, when she'd preceded Cathy down the aisle. The shock of Adam's magnifying presence and stark, handsome face had put a noticeable stutter in her step. Enough that the busybodies had clucked over it, though none had guessed the true reason. They all thought she was regretting the loss of Zack.

"Does he know that Laurel booked herself onto a convenient Mediterranean cruise ship so she wouldn't be in town for the wedding?" Allie said, looking from one woman to the other.

"He knows." Cathy was eyeing Julia with too much sympathy. Now that the mints were gone, Allie was beginning to notice. "Laurel's not what matters."

Allie's lips pursed. "His legs?"

"His legs are fine," Julia insisted. Too much emphasis.

Allie squinched again, her eyes narrowing to slits, her long nose twitching suspiciously.

"You only have to look at him to see." Julia couldn't seem to stop herself. Very unlike her. "He's every bit as vital as he was when he left."

"Vital?" Allie echoed. "Like a daily vitamin?" She chortled. "If I were you, I wouldn't count on Adam sticking around for another dose tomorrow, let alone the long haul."

Julia winced. "If you were me? I—I'm not counting on anything. Which isn't the point, anyway. All I meant—" She took a breath, appalled at herself for losing her cool for so little reason. "Nothing. Forget it."

Cathy stepped in. "Allie, would you gather together the single women? It's time I threw the bouquet." As soon as Allie was out of earshot, she turned to the flustered Julia. "Honey—are you okay? I knew it was going to be hard on you, seeing Adam again."

You don't know the half of it, Julia thought. She clenched her hands, safely hidden in a lapful of tulle netting. Cathy had guessed about Julia's feelings for Adam months ago, when Julia had confessed that—contrary to public speculation—she was not heartbroken over Zack. But Cathy didn't know that there was a lot more to the story.

"Well, sure," Julia said slowly, "I was a little nervous about what to expect. But it turns out that Adam's still Adam."

Cathy laughed. "Is that good or bad? I haven't known him long enough to tell."

Julia mulled it over. He was good for a change—her change—but a mighty bad influence on her usual rock-steady equilibrium. "It's both," she said. "Adam's always been..." She gave a wordless gesture, knowing there was no rhyme or reason for her attraction to the man. Adam Brody was just there—a dream in her head, a knot in her stomach, a longing in her heart.

"Impossible to peg down," Cathy said, nodding. "I like him, though. After hearing all the stories, I thought he'd be one of those careless extreme-sports dudes with the cocky attitudes. But he's not—he's quiet and intelligent, with a dry sense of humor. When I think of all he's been through—" Catching Julia's misting eyes, she broke off. "Ah, but I don't need to tell *you,* do I?"

Julia gave a watery sniff. "At eighteen, he was pretty darn cocky. The Brodys worried like crazy over his daredevil tendencies, and they never even learned about some of the wilder escapades." She thought sadly of the new hesitation about Adam, the look of worry in his eyes that had aged him beyond twenty-eight. "But I suspect he's changed some after the car accident."

"Maybe you'll get the chance to find out?" Cathy gave her a sisterly little nudge.

"Maybe."

"Try to persuade him to stay, will you?"

Julia was going to say that Adam had never before paid any attention to her requests, but just then Allie and a swarm of eager guests arrived, buzzing with excitement over the bridal bouquet and the newlyweds' impending departure. Julia was swept into the celebratory crowd despite her reluctance. She didn't believe in superstition and sentiment—she believed in drawing up a plan and making things happen.

The wedding guests surged out of the restaurant into the gravel parking lot. Zack's black Jaguar was decked out in shaving cream, ribbons of crepe paper, tin cans, pinwheels and the traditional Just Married placard. Julia picked Adam out from the crowd, her heart expanding when she saw the genuine smile on his face. The honey-colored glow of the sunset caught in his moss-green eyes, lighting them up like twin fireflies.

Ten years, she thought, her chest hurting. *I've been feeling like this for ten years. That's long enough.*

Long enough to make even a sane woman ready to jump out of an airplane.

Cathy and Zack stood on the doorstep beneath the deep stone arch of the entrance, looking exactly like the model couple for a wedding cake topper. They hugged Zack's parents and Cathy's dad, Admiral Wallace Winston Bell, then ran toward their getaway vehicle in a shower of flower petals. Cathy paused at the open car door, held up her bouquet to a cheer from the crowd and with a graceful flick of her wrist tossed it high in the air.

The single women jostled for position. Julia followed the bouquet's spinning arc, her hands involuntarily reaching to the sky before she remembered and pulled them in. Gwendolyn Case, a token member of the Heartbroken club even though she'd already been married and divorced twice, made an impressive leap and catch despite the billowing skirts of her size eighteen pumpkin-colored bridesmaid dress and size eleven dyed-to-match pumps. A roar went up from the guests as the admiral swept her up for a big hug and smooch.

As Zack and Cathy drove away in a clatter, Julia met Adam's eyes over the milling crowd. *I don't want a bridal bouquet. I'm as free and easy and daring as you,* she wanted to say, but settled for a little smile of mutual amusement before his extended family of uncles and in-laws and cousins thrice removed descended en masse, blocking him from view.

Poor Adam, she thought, getting an idea.

2

Yes, indeed. Now that she was eighteen and officially legal, making love to Zack was the safe, even expected thing to do. None of their friends would have believed they'd held out this long, considering they'd been going together for two years. Julia wasn't sure why they had delayed, except that she'd always pulled back at the last moment. Losing her virginity was a momentous occasion, and she was a cautious person.

Too cautious, maybe.

"It's now or never," she vowed, but flinched when a knock at the door finally came. How silly. She'd considered the situation very carefully before deciding that Zack was the one. There was no reason to be unsure about letting him in.

It would be okay. Julia put her hand on the knob. Zack was the safe, smart choice. He would take care of her.

"Julia!" The cries went up.

"Girlfriend! You made it! Come and join the party."

"Hot damn, another bridesmaid!"

Adam didn't chime in. Instead he crouched to feed another piece of wood into the bonfire, trying unsuccessfully to keep his eyes off the latest arrival at the impromptu beach party. Julia wore black leggings with low boots and a bulky sweater, her hair pulled straight back from her face. When she turned to accept a beer from Fred, the firelight gilded her profile like the delicate, curved designs on a Chinese vase. She'd always had a way about her—neat, clean, exacting, pedestal pure. Even after he'd ruined it all by touching her.

The flames leaped, devouring the dry wood. He threw on a chunk of punky log. Sparks rose in a glittering curtain. Rocking back on his heels, he watched as they dispersed, finding one glowing fleck that floated high in the dark sky, following a meandering path before finally winking out.

Most of the crowd sat on lawn chairs or beach blankets. Julia passed up a couple of offers, circling the group until she came to Adam. "Have a seat," he said after an awkward moment, aware of her in his peripheral vision even though his gaze remained on the crackling fire.

"Hi." She sat on the old felled log he'd been using as a seat. It had been on this beach for as long as he remembered.

"Hi."

"There's room for two."

The fire wasn't going anywhere. He edged backward until he was perched on the log. Half buried in the sand, it was weathered gray and smooth, all but a few stubborn shreds of bark worn off by countless numbers of beach bums.

"Want a beer?" she said, tilting her bottle.

"I've got one, thanks." He reached for it, tucked out of the way in a fork of the log's broken branches.

The tension between them seemed unbearable. What had happened to his long resolve to treat her as just another of his brother's admirers? It had worked for years, keeping them from exchanging more than the average meaningless chitchat. And stopping him from touching her, except for the occasional quick hug hello or a casual brush of the shoulders or hands or hips.

Had Zack's marriage ripped away the chains?

No. Adam's limbs wouldn't feel so heavy and his reactions so slow if that were the case.

The electric shock zinging through his veins he could ignore if he kept trying.

Julia looped her arms around her knees. "I can't help thinking that Zack should be here," she said softly, keeping their conversation to themselves among the more raucous back-and-forth of the others.

"I miss him, too."

"He's always been the leader of this crowd." She scanned the circle of good friends, laughing and talking in the warm, radiant glow of the fire. "Even with most of us married or moved away, busy with careers and children, we'll always be close. That's what's so special about small towns."

"Is that why you chose to live in Quimby permanently?"

She glanced at him, then quickly away. "Sure. Partly."

He didn't press. He never did—not with Julia. It wouldn't do him any good to know the answers.

Arm's length, he thought. A safe distance. Even though he could feel her, sitting beside him so blamelessly, their legs not quite touching. Her cheek was rosy in the firelight, the smooth sweep of her ponytail honey gold threaded with a rich amber brown. He'd never stopped wanting to touch her hair. Her face. Her throat. Her breasts.

"I was surprised that Zack came back," he said, "after all the trouble with Laurel and the wedding that wasn't." His brother was a good subject to keep between them.

"Oh, no. Zack belongs here."

"Not like me."

Someone had brought a CD player. Fred jumped up and shook his rump—and his beer gut—in an attempt to get Allie to dance around the fire with him. Jeering, she pelted him with corn chips. Through all the noise, Zack heard Julia's quick intake of breath.

"How can you say that?" She leaned closer, looking him full in the face with her hand on his knee. "You belong here as much as anyone."

"I'm no Zack."

She gave a mystified shake of the head. "So what?"

He shrugged. Put that way, he sounded like an idiot. "All I meant was—Zack is more prominent. The leader, like you said. No one would miss me if I stayed away permanently."

Julia lifted her hand off his knee. "I guess not."

Oh.

She took a long drink of the beer, even though he knew she wasn't crazy about the taste. Dabbed her lips with the edge of her sleeve. To show she was aware that he was watching, she gave him a bland smile, deliberately saying nothing more.

He got the point. One, quit whining. Two, don't ask for ego reinforcement from the one woman who had particular reason to notice when he was gone. Even though she couldn't admit it, Julia was as aware of him as he was of her. And that was plenty. Each time he returned home, he scrutinized every detail about her. When they were together, he was continually aware of where she was in proximity to him, who she was talking to, of her every laugh and gesture and smile. He could close his eyes and identify her by smell. Clean and fresh with a hint of sunny lavender. Never cloying.

Better for him to stay away, he thought, feeling desire stirring his gut.

Always the same attraction—and the same conclusion.

"I suppose you'll be leaving soon," she said casually.

He'd been in Idaho far too long—a stay enforced by his accident and slow recovery. As much as he enjoyed the state's rugged outdoor life—the beautiful but treacherous mountains and rivers—he usually craved new experiences before too long. But this past year had been different. Idle and faced with too much time to think, he'd found himself longing not for unseen vistas but for the rolling hills and open farmland of Quimby, his humble hometown.

But that was only because the unknown was out of reach to him now.

Had to be.

"I don't have anywhere to go," he confessed.

Julia showed her surprise. "Oh, pfft. Adam Brody always has somewhere to go."

"No job." Over the years, he'd worked a variety of jobs, from tree surgeon to river guide to sky dive instructor to construction. All of them physical and beyond his present capabilities. "Gave up my lease." First time in his life he'd had a lease—an experience he didn't plan to repeat. "All my meager possessions are packed in the back of my Jeep."

"A sleeping bag, a tent, a mountain bike and a kayak," she said. "A pair of hiking boots and enough rock-climbing equipment to scale the Manhattan skyline."

"That about sums it up." He tilted his head and drained the beer, thinking of two possessions she'd missed—the cane that Zack had kept replacing each time Adam snapped one in frustration and the worn photo that was always buttoned in one of his shirts or jacket pockets. He kept the first under the car seat for the rare times he needed it. The second was Julia on her eighteenth birthday.

"Then you're free to stay for a while." Was that hope in her voice or was he imagining it?

"I wasn't planning on more than a few days."

"Long enough to teach me to rock climb?"

He sent her a slanted smile. "Kinda hoped you'd forgotten about that."

"Nope. I've penciled you into my date book, smack dab between an estate-tax seminar and the Holliwells' open house."

She was kidding. He was sure she was kidding.

Gwendolyn Case came around, passing out hot dogs. Adam took two and chose a twin-pronged stick to roast them on. "You're looking really good," Gwen said, lingering.

"You, too, Gwen." The buxom bridesmaid had put jeans on under her formal dress and bunched the skirts at her waist, strapping them in with a belt. Snagging the bridal bouquet had made her bolder than ever—despite her interest in the admiral, she'd been making a game of sizing up the available choices over the bonfire. Adam's response was perfunctory at best. To him, Gwen would always be the brassy, bossy baby-sitter who'd once wrestled him out of a tree and sat on him till he'd promised not to climb it again.

"Chuck's looking hungry," Julia said.

Gwen spun around, lighting up when she saw that Chuck Cheswick, who was as big as a bear and twice as ravenous, had already finished his third hot dog.

"Sneaky," Adam said when Gwen had gone.

"A woman with a bridal bouquet is a dangerous creature. A few more seconds and you'd have shot to the top of her eligible bachelor list." Julia smoothed a loose strand of hair behind her ear. "You owe me now."

"I can take care of myself," he said, then stopped, feeling uneasy because he'd learned that the statement wasn't always true. He positioned the hot dogs over a chunk of burned log that glowed orange with black edges, good for a slow roast.

"No excuse not to express appreciation for my diversion tactic." Julia's tone was light and teasing, but he could see that she recognized what he was going through. Since the accident, his self-image had taken a serious beating. He still struggled with the adjustment. Against it, truthfully.

He remembered resenting Zack, especially on the days he needed him most. His brother had an easy charm, a large capacity to love and forgive. He also had good fortune, good looks and two good legs. There had been days Adam hated him.

"Leave me alone," he'd said again and again. Sometimes with bitterness, sometimes with fear or twisted pride or weakness. He hadn't wanted anyone, even a brother, to see him that way.

Zack refused. "For once you can't do the leaving, brother. I'm taking advantage of that for as long as I can." And he'd stayed, with never a complaint. As if it had been for his own benefit.

"I can handle this on my own," Adam said when he began physical therapy. Never mind that he was running with sweat, clinging to the bars of a walker as though it tilted on the edge of a precipice.

"Of course you can," Zack said. "I'm just here for the entertainment value. This is better than your teenage Evel Knievel motorcycle act."

Adam cursed him out all the way across the hospital room till he stood panting at the open door.

Zack had applauded. And then said, "Dare you to keep going." He'd known exactly how to treat his prickly brother—with brusque affection and a dare. Adam had never turned down a dare.

"All right, all right," he said now to Julia. "I appreciate you running interference. Just don't expect a reward."

"You're burning the hot dogs."

He pulled them from the flames, waving as the breeze turned and stinging smoke billowed into their faces. "I am not teaching you to rock climb."

She squinted. "Yes, you are." She folded a bun around one of the charred wieners and slid it off the stick. Then the other. "Ketchup, mustard?" she asked, flicking through the packets of condiments that were being passed around the circle. "Relish?"

He stabbed the stick into the sand, digging into the cool grains with his knuckles. "Why should I?"

Carefully she squeezed ketchup over the hot dog balanced on her kneecaps. "Because..." She licked her thumb, looking at Adam from the corners of her eyes. Other noises seemed to recede until he heard only the sound of the lake lapping at the shore, the gentle swish of evergreen branches brushing against each other.

"Because I have something you need." Julia's voice was soft, seductive—and as much a part of him as the infinite sky and the flow of water and the silken sand that ran through his fingers faster than before.

Life is short, he'd learned.

Grab her while you can.

THEY ATE HOT DOGS, they talked briefly about Zack and Cathy—whom he really didn't know at all except that he liked her for not fussing at him for coming late to her wedding—and they joined in a dozen conversations except their own. Adam began to feel easier about being home now that he was past the humps of gossip and open speculation.

"You haven't changed at all," one of the women said resentfully when he'd repeated his plan to depart as soon as possible. They were all suddenly interested in knowing what he was doing next. He was operating under the assumption that saying it out loud would make it so, even if he didn't know where to go or what to do.

Julia smiled a little at that. Secretively. As if she had plans for him. He waited for a spurt of annoyance, but it never came. A prickle of anticipation did.

Eventually one of the guys brought out a guitar, and the music lulled the group into a lazy mood. They sang a few folk songs. Hokey stuff, but he liked it. Julia's eyes were luminescent, giving him a pleasant jolt each time he intercepted her gaze. He resisted the urge to put his arm around her.

The guitarist played several popular Fleetwood Mac songs and then "Landslide." A number of the circle sang along until gradually their voices dropped away and only Julia was left. Her voice was smooth and clear as she sang about seasons and changes and reflections in the snow-covered hills. Adam looked at her until the ache in his throat was too much and then he closed his eyes and swallowed hard, unable to stop wanting this to go on forever—Julia's sweet voice, the strumming guitar, the riveting contrast of cool night and hot flame. And, for once, no restlessness rankling inside him.

Eventually the song ended with a smattering of applause, signaling the end of the evening. The group began to break up. Julia blinked and tucked the stray strand behind her ear again, hesitating for a moment before hopping to her feet. She stuck out her hand to Adam. "Come with me. I have something to show you. And if you're very good, I'll even let you have it."

HE'D INSISTED on taking her in his Jeep. The practical side of her kept pointing out that it would have made more sense for her to lead in her own car, but when did Adam Brody ever listen to sense? To his senses, sure, all the time. But to sense—common sense? Average people didn't throw themselves off cliffs and out of airplanes in their spare time.

His mother used to say, wringing her hands over his most recent white-water or skydiving adventure, "That boy spent all his common cents years ago." Whereas Julia had always counted her piggy-bank savings down to the exact penny, knowing in advance exactly where and on what she would spend them, practical soul that she was.

"Penny for your thoughts," Adam said, following her directions to veer off the highway onto a newly paved road that led to the other side of Mirror Lake.

She laughed at the coincidence. "I was thinking that I probably shouldn't bring you here. Your mom won't like it. She wants you home to stay."

"I'm never home to stay."

"True." Julia clutched the door handle, her stomach flip-flopping. Adam wouldn't stay, no matter what. All she could hope was to prolong his visit by making it slightly more comfortable. "I hear your house is overrun with relatives."

"Don't remind me." Adam whipped the Jeep around a tight turn. The road curved sharply through the thick forest before the vista opened to a cleared section overlooking the eastern end of the lake. He slowed the vehicle drastically at the sight of raw land. "What happened here?"

"It's a new development." She indicated the large, flagged sign that announced the project. Evergreen Point, Coming Soon.

She hadn't counted on the look of devastation on Adam's face. "I used to camp in these woods," he said. The Jeep crawled along one of the new roads that wound past rows of homes under construction. Other areas were marked with surveyor's stakes. "Jeez."

"I thought you might need a place away from the Brody crowds."

He looked askance. "You're trying to sell me a house?"

"No! Of course not. But I am the listing agent for this development. I have keys to the model home." A bad idea, she thought. He'd sooner pitch a tent in a mall parking lot. "If you wanted to use it," she said haltingly. "Just to, you know, get away...."

Julia stopped and took a breath. What was wrong with her? She was unflappable; everyone said so.

Adam touched the brakes and turned to look at her. "What are you saying?"

"I'm offering you the use of the model home. At night. You'd have to clear out during working hours. There's lots of construction going on, and I have clients to show through the house."

"Sneaky," he said, raising his brows. "This isn't like the Goldie I remember. She always followed the rules."

Heat crawled up Julia's throat. "Maybe you don't know me as well as you think."

"Guess not. Skydiving, rock climbing, housebreaking. What's next?"

"This is a straight-up swap. I give you a place to stay, you give me rock-climbing lessons." She unsnapped her seat belt, eager to get away from his open curiosity. "Are you interested? Shall we take a look?"

"Why not?"

"You might even like it." He followed her through the most advanced section of the development. Even so, it was like a ghost town—gaping windows, bare bones of new walls, utter silence.

Beyond the lots, the lake glistened, black onyx dappled with silver moonlight. She might have been wrong about the house, but Julia was certain that the desolation would appeal to Adam.

The model home was one of several that were finished, the only one furnished and decorated. It was a large house with a two-story entry and living room. The vast proportions should appeal, as well—Adam could never live in a box.

She took the keys from her purse as they followed the newly laid herringbone brick walk to the front door. "Solid construction," she said, letting them inside. "Good design. Built to stock plans, but the builders hired Zack to modify the blueprints so each house will be unique."

"No need to sell me." Adam's glance skated across the plush furnishings and went straight to the clerestory windows. Tiny stars dotted the strip of visible sky.

"Sorry. Automatic response." Regret gripped her. Suddenly it was clear-cut. This wasn't Adam's kind of place. "You hate it, don't you?"

He eyed the pristine decor, the sparkling whiteness of the walls. "It's straight from the pages of a glossy magazine. I'd be afraid of messing things up."

"Ha. I know you. You wouldn't leave a crumb." He might be reckless with his life, but he was surgically precise in his mode of living. Even tonight, at the bonfire, he'd been the last to leave, tending to the fire pit and sweeping the area free of debris. She'd always thought he was like a night creature lurking in the woods—silent and swift, leaving nary a broken twig or an overturned leaf behind as he passed by. Not one sign that he'd been there.

Except for me, she thought. *Inside me.* She'd always remember.

"It's just a place to sleep," she said, surprised at the roughness of her voice. "You don't have to like it."

"Thanks for the offer, but it gives me the creeps." He walked out the open door without looking back.

"You didn't even go upstairs. There's a cupola." She hurried after him. "You like heights, don't you? You could bunk down in the cupola. There's a great view of the lake from up there."

He turned and scanned the roof. "It's all glassed in." Playfully, he put his hands around his neck to simulate choking. "Ever read *The Bell Jar*?"

Not a joke, although he acted as if it were. At times she wondered if he was claustrophobic. He disliked the indoors more than anyone this side of a South Seas islander, which was why the months after his accident must have been a living hell as much for the confinement as for the threat of paraplegia.

"I suppose you can go back to your parents' house," she commented, light as air. "Who's sharing your bedroom again?"

After a moment, Adam smiled. "My cousin Jack. The one with asthma and the suitcase full of medicine bottles. His vaporizer whistles all night long."

Wordlessly, Julia held the key to him.

He put out his palm to catch it.

Her impulse was to grab his hand in both of hers, to hold it against her cheek as she folded the key into his palm and pressed kisses over his knuckles. He had artistic hands—long-fingered, nimble, hardened with calluses but ultrasensitive to stimuli. Another little fact about him that she'd filed away in her memory banks for warm dreams on long, cold, lonely winter nights.

But now was not the time to get seriously kissy-faced with his hands. Skilled at turning back her impulses, she dropped the key and stepped away without betraying even one emotion, certain she'd pushed far enough for one night. It wouldn't do for Adam to guess her feelings so soon when he'd probably put her out of his mind years ago.

No, he hasn't, an inner voice told her, but it was small and quiet and easy to overlook.

Adam slipped the key into the pocket of his black tuxedo pants before gesturing at one of the unfinished structures. "Now, that, Goldie, is more my speed."

"You can't go there," she said, but he was already gone. She rushed to catch up, her low-heeled boots pounding the dirt. "Adam, no." She stepped over a pile of bricks. "It's dangerous."

He looked at her and smiled, and that was when she knew what she should have done was bonk at least one of them over the head with the closest two-by-four.

Because dangerous was Adam's middle name.

The house's walls were up and wrapped in Tyvek, the roof partly shingled. The interior was a hollow shell, whistling with the wind that came in through a couple of openings that weren't yet glassed in. Their footsteps rang on the plywood subfloor as she followed him to a makeshift staircase that any self-respecting carpenter would have called a ladder.

"Careful," she whispered. There was no handrail.

"Stay downstairs," he said. "I'll take just a quick look."

"I'm coming." She tromped up the steep stairs without looking down. Looking down wouldn't get her anywhere. Her whole life had been spent checking for stumbling blocks because homecoming queens weren't supposed to fall on their faces. Enough was enough. She wanted to step outside the box and really live.

Adam gave her his hand to help her up the last steps, and that was good because she could blame the gnawing in her stomach on their chemistry instead of queasiness. One quick survey of the second floor and she knew for certain what he was going to do. And that if she were to keep up, she'd have to follow him. "You can't possibly mean to—"

He did. The house had a cupola similar to the other, except this one was unfinished. Open stud frame, no glass, no stairs, not even a ladder. "Think of the view," Adam said as he poked his head out the huge hole that would eventually be filled with the master bedroom's picture window.

She gripped the ledge, taking a quick glance before backing away. "The view's fine from right here." Dark water glinted through the heavy fringe of the pine forest.

"You can't see over the trees." He leaned farther. She nearly grabbed for his belt, but he wasn't wearing one. Only thin black suspenders over the pleated tuxedo shirt, its collar open and the sleeves shoved up to his elbows. James Bond after a mission, devastatingly sexy in his throwaway glamour.

"What's the point?" she nearly wailed when Adam climbed onto the window ledge. For a man who'd seemed unsure of his physical abilities, he was tremendously limber.

Crouching, he threw a glance over his shoulder, calming her with his easy bravado. His face had lost the serious cast that she found so worrisome. "You know what they say about Everest. Because it's there." He gave her a boyish, lopsided grin and then leaped like a cat.

She let out an "Eep!" and rushed to the window in time to see Adam's dangling legs disappear over the eaves. Apparently he'd used a trim board as a step, but she didn't want to think of how he'd hoisted himself over the edge. There was no way she could follow.

Staring intently at the slanted ceiling, she listened for his footsteps, hearing nothing until he stuck his head out of the gap where the cupola stairs would go. "Over here."

She circled beneath him, craning her neck and kicking up sawdust. "You've done this sort of thing before, haven't you?"

"Remember the abandoned barn on Old Town Road? I used to swing out the haymow on a rope and walk the peak of the roof to get to the cupola."

"Figures." She rocked on her heels. "I hope the view is worth it." Upside down, his face was still compelling. Even more so because now every shred of reserve was gone. This was the Adam Brody she remembered. For once, she understood the attraction of conquering the unconquerable obstacle. For that, she was glad she'd brought him here.

"Want to see?" He extended an arm, waggling his fingers at her.

She reached, knowing it was useless. Six feet of empty space separated them. "There's no way."

"You said you wanted to climb." The reversed position had reddened his hollow cheeks. "Dare you."

Adam and his friends had always flung dares around like chicken feed. As Miss Prim and Proper, popularity on a pedestal, she'd never been included.

No way was she turning her first one down.

She looked around the room, finding it littered with various building supplies. Sacks of plaster made an untidy pile against the side wall. "Maybe there's scaffolding or a ladder," she said, wishing—absurdly, but since when had her interest in this man ever been sensible?—that for once she could join Adam in midair. "Send in the clowns," she muttered to herself, grunting as she rearranged the heavy sacks. One of them toppled off the precarious pile, landing with a thud and a puff of white dust.

"I'm coming down," Adam said, briefly disappearing before his legs swung into the gap.

"No—stay there!" Julia climbed to the top of the stack and balanced with her arms out to her sides, biting her lip with determination. Suddenly it was very important that she get up on the roof. "I'm coming up."

But not nearly high enough. She'd made up four feet, at best. Until Adam swung around again, going prone with his entire upper body hanging from the gap. They were able to clasp hands. "This doesn't help," she gasped, except that it did. His sure grip steadied her footing. She stretched higher, wrapping her hands around his forearms like a trapeze artist, and suddenly felt herself rising toward the ceiling.

The strain must have been incredible on Adam's shoulders. For one instant, right before he pulled her the last bit and her elbows landed on solid wood, she wondered if his muscles would give out. He was using his legs as much as his arms; they were hooked around one of the cupola's support posts, anchoring both their weights.

"Oof." The lip of the staircase opening bit into her midsection as he grabbed her by the waist and the rear end and hauled her bodily onto the platform. They collapsed, breathing hard. The smell of fresh sawn wood was strong in the air. "What was that?" she gasped, her pulse hammering. "The Flying Wallendas?" She lifted a limp hand, let it fall. "You're strong. I didn't know you were so strong."

He blew out a big breath. "I'm deceptively wiry."

They propped themselves on their elbows. She looked warily around the framed but not enclosed cupola. It was like being in an open-air cage perched high among the treetops. Although the roof was on, she could see the stars between the studs of the open walls. "How will we get down?"

"Going down is always easier than getting up."

"Not when you're a trapeze artist." She peered over the edge, then past the slope of the roof to the hard bare ground. It was a long drop. "No safety net, either."

With a concentrated look on his face, Adam got slowly to his feet. "Risks don't come with safety nets, Goldie. Quit worrying and get up to admire the view." His hand went around her elbow as he helped her stand. She swore she felt each one of his fingertips press hotly into her flesh right through her thick sweater, as if the half-inch of wool was no more than a wisp of silk. Then his arm wound around her, setting her waist afire. Her hairline began to perspire. The stars danced in the sky. For a few wonderful moments, she remembered what it had been like to have his hands on her—everywhere.

Casually, he took his arm away. But she saw how he gripped the raw wood sash, his eyes aimed at the view of Mirror Lake.

The wind caught her hair. She smoothed it, licking her parched lips. "Well. This is pretty nice."

"Worth risking your life?"

"I'm not saying that."

"Then why the hell do you want to scale a mountain or jump out of a plane?"

Julia felt as though all her acceptable notions were in upheaval, crashing and colliding inside her head like tectonic plates, made even more tumultuous by Adam's presence. She'd said she wanted change. But change equaled Adam, and Adam equaled heartache, because she knew, she just *knew* that he would leave. It was what had always stopped her before, the idea of being left in Quimby with a whole lot of pleasant nothingness stretched before her. Nothing but memories.

"Because I..." She filled her lungs with the sweet night air, her gaze glued to the far shore, where the glistening blue-black of the lake met the dense green-black of the trees. It was a conundrum. Did she want nothing but memories, or memories of nothing?

Just jump, she thought, and so she did.

"Because, aside from the physical challenge, I want you—" A metaphorical wind whistled past her ears. "I want to be with you and see if we—if we—" *Here comes the thud.* "If we might still have feelings for each other."

A deep silence encased her, hollow as a well, stifling as a bell jar.

Julia's instincts for self-preservation screamed inside

her head. Adam had probably dared her up to the cupola to show her that she was not capable of feats of derring-do. But he'd miscalculated. She'd done it, and now she was taking another flying leap, risking more than a hard landing.

Broken bones heal, you goose. Hearts don't—not as easily.

She remembered Cathy saying that the Brody spell lasted a long time. It was true. Julia had been wanting to try again with Adam ever since her eighteenth birthday—the night they didn't talk about because to do so would be to acknowledge a major betrayal of trust.

It had been ten years. Long years. Other than the aberration of his involvement with Laurel, Adam's asceticism had been known to reach monklike proportions. Julia had tried to be as disciplined, but she wasn't. She was human and frail and filled with yearnings for what she couldn't forget.

The terrible silence continued.

She looked at Adam crosswise. His hard-edged profile was inscrutable.

He's all bone, she thought. *Bone and sinew and tough muscle. No softness at all...or is there?* Buried deep beneath the bravado and the austerity and the iron will, was there maybe a soft spot for her? The tiniest bit of tenderness?

She thought there might be. Was counting on it, in fact.

All I want is a safe place to land, she told herself.

Which was such a lie, but a lie she'd better darn well stick to.

3

"ADAM?"

"Julia?" Adam stared in shock. "What are you doing here?"

"I'm—it's—" Julia clutched the lapel of a loose, shimmery robe beneath her chin—she sure hadn't been wearing that last time he'd seen her—and glanced over her shoulder at the candlelit motel room. He tried not to gape at the way her breasts moved beneath the silk. "I wasn't expecting y-you. I was expecting...." Her voice died as she backed away, flushing pink with embarrassment.

Zack. Of course, Adam thought. She didn't want him. She wanted Zack.

The sound of an approaching car made Julia rush forward. She grabbed his hand and pulled him into the room, then slammed the door. "Isn't Zack coming?"

"I don't know. I got this note—" Adam reached into his shirt pocket, making sure to withdraw the note and not the photograph he'd filched from the party.

Julia snatched it from his hand, her eyes wild. Wilder than he'd ever seen them. "Who gave this to you?"

"One of the guys. The party was breaking up and someone said Fred left this for me. Didn't make sense, but..." Adam shrugged. In her distress, Julia had forgotten about the robe. And the short gown she wore under it. Her legs were bare,

and the rest of her, too, he'd bet, beneath the not-quite-sheer silk.

Abruptly, Adam sat on the bed. Oh, man. He was hard. She'd see. And be horrified, because she was his brother's girlfriend and he wasn't supposed to think about her that way.

Julia was staring at the crumpled note, her long blond hair falling against her cheeks.

Adam cleared his throat. "You got the wrong brother, huh?"

AT FIRST, Adam refused to look at her. "Did you know I went to Japan?"

She gave a wordless gesture, apparently thrown by the non sequitur.

"Three years ago." His heart was racing at a ridiculous pace.

"I heard about it secondhand," she said, brittle-voiced.

"It was a memorable trip. I went to do some ice climbing in Hokkaido, but I ended up staying for six months. Their philosophy of living in harmony with nature is inspiring. I hadn't thought the Japanese way of bringing order to the outdoors would appeal to me, but it did. Have you ever seen a Japanese garden? Absolute perfection. There are people whose job it is to pick shreds of debris from the great moss gardens—painstaking hours spent on their hands and knees..."

She wrinkled her nose. "And you've decided it's your calling to be one of them?"

"God, no. They'd have to take me away in a straitjacket by the end of the first working day."

Julia leaned her cheek against one of the support

beams. "Then what are you trying to tell me?" Her bangs ruffled in the wind, and she hunched her shoulders, wrapping her arms around herself. Her wounded air knifed him.

"I traveled throughout the country, sleeping on tatami, eating rice and fish and seaweed. One day in a tiny village in the alps I met a craftsman who carved wooden bowls and boxes. He was ancient, could barely move his fingers, and still he was working to carve a vessel without flaw. He'd dedicated his life to the pursuit of perfection."

"There's no such thing."

"No? Isn't a—" Wind swirled through the oak and maple trees, rattling the dry brown leaves. "Isn't a leaf perfection?"

Julia shook her head. "I've spent hours looking for the perfect autumn leaf to press. There are always minute flaws."

"A rock?" he said, reaching into his pants pocket.

Her lashes dropped as he held his hand out to her, knuckles up. Freeing her arms, she stuck out a hand that was nearly enveloped by her sweater sleeve. He gently unfurled her fingers, then dropped a small rock into her palm and closed her fingers over it. "Don't look." She was so still he could hear the soft sound of her breathing. Maybe her heartbeat. "Touch. It's perfect."

Her eyes closed in concentration. The stone was rounded, worn smooth by time. He watched her turn it over and over in her palm, her fingertips caressing the texture, perhaps feeling for flaws. But she didn't look.

"It's my habit to pick up a rock everywhere I travel. A

chip of shale. An agate washed up on the shore. Ordinary river rocks from every river I've rafted..."

She parted her lips with the tip of her tongue. "Why?"

"Mementos, I suppose."

With her eyes still closed, she brought the rock to her mouth as if she intended to kiss it. His pulse stutter-stepped, but instead she ran the stone back and forth across her lower lip, continuing to test for imperfections. "And this one?"

"Idaho."

Moonlight emphasized the gold cast of her hazel eyes when she looked sideways at him. It bathed the soft curves of her cheeks and chin and lips. Crazy moon.

"There's more to the story," she whispered, turning the rock in her fingers again as she studied it. A soft inhale. "Oh. A flaw." Her thumb rubbed against the stain that marred the smooth gray surface.

"Blood," he said.

She flinched. The stone jumped from her fingertips. With a tiny thud, it landed on the roof below them and rolled down the slope, disappearing into the blackness.

"Oh, no!" Julia leaned over the frame of the window opening, extending an arm as if she could reach to the ground. "I'm so sorry, Adam. We can climb down and find it—"

He put his hand on her shoulder to draw her back. "No. Let it go." *Time to let it go.*

"But..." She rubbed her mouth with a ribbed sweater sleeve. "Blood? Whose?"

"My own."

Her face turned toward his, stricken with emotion. "Adam...how awful."

So he told her about his car wreck, how through his own recklessness he'd lost control, rebounded off the oncoming van and flipped over the guardrail. He'd been thrown from the car. For an eternity he'd clung precariously to the side of the mountain, broken and twisted, clutching at dirt and roots and rocks, making wild promises to God—pledges to never take a risk again—that went against all that he was. Once he'd been rescued and sent to the hospital, a nurse had pried the stone from his fist and saved it to give to Zack for Adam.

"A year later, I went back to the site of the accident. I meant to throw the rock away. But I couldn't."

Julia's teeth were gritted, her hands clenched on the windowsill. "And now I've lost it."

He resisted the urge to tuck the stray strand of hair behind her ear. "It doesn't matter. I'm finished with it."

Her eyes flashed in the moonlight, a sheen of wet gold. "Are you really?"

Was he? "I think I am."

She flexed her fingers before putting her hand on his arm. "Why now and not before?"

"Because I'm home," he said without thinking.

"Not to stay." Conflicting reactions warred in her voice, but caution was winning. Her eyes were round and wary, the light touch of her hand as heavy as stone to him. "You're in pursuit of your own perfection. It's a fierce, terrible kind of perfection." She gave his sleeve a little tug, then released him as she turned away, restlessly smoothing her hair. "And it frightens me."

Me, too, he thought.

His flaw.

HE DROPPED DOWN through the stairwell opening, then stood on the stacked burlap sacks to catch her dangling body and ease her to the floor, every male instinct roused by the intimacy of holding her tight against himself, her rounded bottom nestled to his groin in a perfect fit. She didn't say a word, and neither did he, avoiding looking too closely at the flush of her cheeks as he drove her to the beach for her car. He let out a big breath of relief after she drove away, amazed that he'd managed to avoid answering her question about exploring their relationship. If he intended to see her again, though, he'd have to come up with something. There must be a good reason they shouldn't act on the combustible feelings between them, and he would use it when next they met. Safer all around, he thought, ignoring the streak inside him that rebelled at the notion of playing it safe. He could do it for Julia's sake. She might think she wanted risk, but she didn't, really, no more than she needed a man like him. She was cut out for a regular life as a regular wife, that was patently obvious and always had been. He repeated it once more to himself as he drove home to check in with his parents because they would notice if he didn't return, and he'd given them enough grief to last a lifetime.

Although he hadn't intended to use Julia's key, at least not that night, he came awake in the deep, mean, black hours of the morning when there is no light in the sky. The weight of the house and all its inhabitants sat on his chest like an anvil as he lay perfectly still in his cramped room under the eaves, listening to the rasp of air in his cousin Jack's swollen nasal passages and the matching wheeze of the vaporizer. *The key,* he thought as all oxygen seeped from his compressed lungs. *The stone.*

Fifteen minutes later he was kneeling at the foundation of the unfinished house, running his fingertips along the overturned earth. He found the stone by touch, knowing it by the weight and feel of it nestled in his cupped palm as he sat with his stiff back pressed against the cold cement blocks of the foundation, his legs stretched before him. He stayed there till dawn lightened the horizon to a burned-charcoal red, breathing deeply while he lingered over his mental snapshots of Julia—from the golden-haired dream girl of his adolescence to the smart, classy woman she was now, the one he couldn't risk knowing too well. By the time the eastern sky was a dusky pink and the birds had begun to sing in the trees, he could see well enough to examine the items that had brought him through the night. In his right hand was the lodestone and in his left the photo of Julia on her birthday, laughing as she blew out the candles on a cake. Julia, perfect and pure.

ADAM WENT HOME with the rising sun, watching as the street lamps winked out one by one. The Brody house was a graceful white wood-frame structure on Curran Street, a glowing sugar cube in the morning light. He let himself in through the back door, then silently moved about the kitchen, putting on the teakettle and measuring out water and grounds to fill the industrial-size coffee urn his mother took up from the basement for family occasions. By the time the coffee was brewed, his father was awake. Adam poured him a cup. They sat together at the kitchen table.

"You've been out already," Reuben Brody said, his bristly chin propped on his hand. Never an Adonis, he seemed to get shorter and skinnier with each passing year. His homely face looked decidedly bleary, his sparse gray hair stuck up at all angles, and the morning blahs weighted the pouches of skin that sagged below his eyes.

But appearances were deceiving. Adam knew his father was sharp at any hour. "Couldn't sleep," he said. "The house was too warm."

"You never change. Many mornings I'd find you, curled up beneath the rhododendron bush with only a blanket. Your mother started locking the doors, but you always discovered the key."

"Or went out the window."

"Can you stay this time?"

Adam dipped a tea bag in and out of his cup of hot water. "For a while."

"We miss you."

"I know. I miss you and Mom, too. I'm sorry I cut my visit to Florida short. I didn't like it there. The air was too heavy. It felt like a warm wet washcloth on my skin." His parents had been living in Key Biscayne for the past year, barring a lengthy stay in Twin Falls during the first months of his recuperation. When he was well enough to travel, he'd gone to visit them at their insistence. Once. Briefly.

"Well, looks like we're back in Quimby to stay," his father said. The news of Zack's wedding had been the excuse they'd been waiting for to return home in glory instead of the ignominy they'd faced when he'd been known as the scandalous jilter of brides.

It was hard on parents when both sons went bad. Adam drank half his tea at once, preferring it to be just a few degrees below burn-your-tongue temperature.

"Your mother's planning to revive the Quimby Independents and run for mayor. Says the town fell to ruins while she was gone. Why not stick around for a while and help her out with the campaign? Through the holidays, at least."

"Thanksgiving," Adam bargained.

"Christmas," Reuben said. "Think of how happy that would make your dear ma."

"She'll have a new daughter-in-law and an entire town to keep her occupied." Eve Brody was an active woman, always looking for stimulation. She was forever latching on to projects. Her husband was more laid-back, taking life in stride instead of rushing ahead to hurry it along. In nature, Adam was like his mother and Zack like his father, though the opposite was true in physical appearance. Zack and Eve possessed stunning good looks.

Reuben had been eyeing his son with deliberate contemplation. "We'll have to find you a similar preoccupation."

"I'm not into politics." Adam got up quickly and splashed the remainder of his tea into the sink. The floor was creaking overhead; water was running in the pipes. Soon the kitchen would be stuffed with Brodys and permutations of Brodys and, even worse, Brody in-laws.

"I wasn't speaking of politics," Reuben said as he

opened the refrigerator and took out a carton of eggs, then on reflection, a second. "Unless you mean sexual politics."

Adam gave his father a brief smile. "We're not allowed to talk about sex at the kitchen table." Their mother had made it a rule after the boys had begun asking embarrassingly frank questions over dinner. Things like, "But how does it get *in* there?"

"Marriage—" his father began.

"—is a lifelong commitment," Adam finished. "If you and Mom are thinking about grandchildren, never fear. Zack will provide." Good old Zack always filled in for the gaps of his younger brother's carefree lifestyle.

"I was thinking of your happiness, son. Want to reach for that mixing bowl—the big one?"

Adam stretched for the top shelf, glad for the distraction.

"Stick around for pancakes?" his father asked, cracking eggs.

"You know I don't eat that heavy stuff."

"I'll let you special order an egg-white omelette."

"No thanks, Dad." Adam rubbed his chin, wishing he'd thought to get his shaving kit while the houseguests were still asleep. By his calculations, he had less than a minute to get out of the house before the onslaught of the hungering hordes. "I've got somewhere to go."

Reuben's head cocked, his gaunt face brightening. "Here comes your mother." Apparently he was able to pick Eve's light footfall out of the avalanche of advancing thuds.

"I'll see her later," Adam said, slipping out the back door.

"Don't forget to return your tux! It's due back by noon."

Adam popped open the screen door and looked inside. "It's upstairs. Do it for me, Dad? Please?"

Reuben lifted his whisk, letting glops of batter fall into the bowl. "Only if you promise to show up for dinner on time tonight, son. Bring Julia. We never see her anymore."

Adam blinked. "How did you—" He shook his head. "I'll see." *I'll see if she'll still talk to me after I talk to her.*

He drove off in the Jeep, in such a rush to leave he squealed the tires. He was not nearly as eager to reach his destination because of what he must say to Julia. On the surface, dating her seemed like a reasonable action. Under the surface, however, lurked all manner of complications. The foremost of which was him hurting her when he said sayonara.

Julia lived in style, as befit Quimby's smartest Realtor. Her home on the eastern end of town sat on the crest of a ridge, overlooking a sweep of rolling pasture on one side and a steep, forested ravine on the other. It looked like a bland little ranch house from the front, very well kept with a gray-and-cream color scheme, a patch of trimmed lawn and a paved drive that led to a two-car garage. Thoroughly conventional. It was on the other side of the front door—which was painted a bright, shiny sky blue—that the surprise came. The back side of the house was all glass, three levels cut into the hillside with a stunning view of the steep green glade and the trickling creek at its bottom.

When Adam rang the doorbell she shouted, "Come in," from somewhere inside. He'd been here twice before, with a group on both occasions—safety in numbers—so he was prepared for the drama of stepping inside the front door to a balcony that opened to nothing but space and glass and the nearly vertical vista. At this time of year, Julia's ravine had gone more gold than green, with most of the leaves fallen off the trees to blanket the hillside in a layer of yellow and brown. The slender gray and silver trunks and their calligraphic tracery of branches outlined a brilliant blue sky. It was a snapping day.

Adam wished he felt ready to meet it on an equal footing.

"In here," Julia said from the right. The kitchen and the formal dining room flanked the top floor's open loft space. A large open living room took up all of the middle level, with the bedrooms at the bottom.

He hesitated. "It's Adam."

She said, "I know."

His footsteps sounded clipped on the hard, shining granite floor. The kitchen was as efficient as its owner—uncluttered blue tile countertops, simple birch cabinets, shiny copper pans hanging from a rack. Everything precisely in its place. Julia even managed to cook without making a mess. It occurred to Adam that the house was not unlike the way he might live—if he had possessions and could stomach staying in one place.

"Good morning. I'm making oatmeal." There was not a utensil in sight. She opened the glass door of a hutch and took out two bowls from an array of blue-and-white china, then silently slid open a drawer with one fingertip and withdrew two pearl-handled spoons and put them on the round white pedestal table that sat before the floor-to-ceiling windows. "Brown sugar," she said, and added a matching sugar bowl to the arrangement.

Either she wasn't surprised to see him or she was hiding it very well. The microwave beeped, and she bustled away before he could say anything.

She apportioned the thick steaming cereal into the bowls. "A stick-to-the-ribs breakfast seemed like the thing for rock climbing."

"But I—"

"It was no trouble to cancel my appointments. There were only two. Please sit down. I wouldn't feel right eating alone."

"I had breakfast at home. I only came to—"

"Just tea, I'll bet." She aimed an oblivious smile at him. "Don't worry. I certainly don't expect my first lesson to last very long. It will be over before you know it."

"You're determined," he said, sitting at last.

"Did you go back to the house at Evergreen Point last night?" She fitted her lips around a heaping spoonful of oatmeal.

"As a matter of fact..."

"Then the bargain is struck."

What could he say?

They finished the oatmeal quickly. Julia whisked the table clear, putting everything directly into the dishwasher and wiping down the gleaming surfaces with a sponge. She was treating him with a brisk geniality that should have made it easier to bring up the just-friends speech. But it didn't.

"About last night," he said, feeling as though gravel had been shoveled down his throat instead of raisin-studded oatmeal.

"Last night was—was..." Julia faltered for an instant. "A singular exception," she finished, too brightly, her gaze fixed six inches above his head.

"Meaning?"

"Meaning you can forget it. Blame it on bridesmaid syndrome."

"I'm not familiar with the symptoms."

"Weddings." Nervously she ran her thumb and forefinger up and down the seams on her denim-clad thighs. "They make women crazy. Particularly the attendants, who are too close to the action to avoid contamination."

He cocked a brow. "Contamination?"

"The dread white-lace disease. It leads to uncommon desperation even in the most levelheaded of women. Like me. Disregard everything I said yesterday."

"I see. You didn't mean any of it?"

She shook her head.

He rose. "Then I'm free to go?"

That startled her. "Wait! I didn't mean that part of it."

"Which part, then?" She looked at him balefully. "We need to get this straight," he insisted, finding it easier to make her say it than to say it himself. What a coward he was.

She sucked in a breath, her nostrils flaring. "We're keeping this—us—just friends," she said. "All right? Just friends. No exploration of uncharted territories."

Uncharted, yes, but not completely unexplored... though now was not the time to bring that up. Or to remember the way she'd once moved so sinuously beneath him. "I can live with that," he said, wondering why he wasn't as relieved as he ought to be. It was what he wanted, wasn't it?

Ha. Definitely not what he wanted. But what was right.

He watched her as she went to the foyer closet and took out a shoe box that held a brand-new pair of rock-climbing shoes. She put on a light suede jacket, stuffing a narrow cashmere scarf and a pair of leather gloves into its pockets. Her beauty was innate—strong and unselfish and decent. She seemed right to him in every way. Nothing new in that.

It was he who was wrong.

"REACH AS FAR as you can with your right hand," Adam called from below.

"I'm reaching...."

"The handhold's there. Do the pincher."

"There's nothing to pinch." She pulled back her arm, scraping her splayed fingers spread across the rough surface of the rock for reassurance. Her left arm took most of her weight, resting on a shelf cut into the rock face. Her footing felt fairly secure—if you could call a slanted six-inch ledge secure. Adam did, of course. But then Adam also thought that she was going to pinch onto a minute bump in the rock and pull herself up by her fingertips.

"It's very nice and homey here," she hollered. "I think I'll stay for a while."

"The longer you do, the harder it will be to move on."

She risked a glance past her shoulder. Adam stood in

the long grass at the base of the granite bluff, looking at her while he kept a firm hold on the belay line. She could still see the whites of his eyes. Damn. She hadn't come near as far as she'd hoped.

"Break's over," he said. "Now slide your right foot higher. As high as it will go. Your rubber soles are going to grip the rock, so don't worry about slipping."

She inched her foot along the narrowing ledge until her knee was practically knocking her chin.

"Now—push up and reach."

She reached, closing her eyes as the muscles in her shoulder and back pulled taut. Her fingertips brushed across an irregularity in the stone. That couldn't be it.

"That's it," Adam called. "Go for it. Pull yourself up."

Her fingertips grabbed on to the ridiculously small handhold. Spread-eagled, she rested her forehead against the granite and intoned, "I respect the rock. I feel the rock. I am the rock," while gathering herself to make the Herculean effort to let go of her safe nook and propel herself upward. *Risk it,* she said inside, and somehow she did. Her left knee banged against the hard surface as she scrambled, pebbles scattering in her frantic search for somewhere to place her foot. A shallow crack ran through the rock face where a dark gray stone intersected the chalky red granite. She wedged the fingers of her left hand into it as Adam had demonstrated, amazingly grateful for what three seconds ago had seemed like an impossible perch.

"Keep going," Adam the tyrant encouraged. "Use your legs."

Ha. Her left leg was hanging loose with nowhere to go.

"How?" she yelled, her cheek plastered to stone.

"Figure it out."

She put the toe of her flexible shoe in the crack, but it slipped out as soon as she shifted. The ball of her foot skidded over the rock, the carabiners on her harness and ropes jangling. "I can't," she said, whispering the words beneath what was left of her breath because Adam had drilled it into her head that she wasn't to say *I can't.*

His voice drifted to her, encouraging. "You can."

She stabbed the toe of her shoe into the fissure. Forget it. She was going to fall.

"This is the toughest section. Make it past here, and you're home free."

"That's what you said ten feet ago," she muttered, recognizing the ploy. The carrot before the mule.

Her muscles were aching something fierce. Would she rather go up or would she rather go down? Adam had made her purposely fall once at the beginning, so she could feel how the safety line threaded through her belt and his figure-eight belaying device would catch her before she dropped. The top line dangled before her, anchored at the crown of the bluff. She turned her face to the other side, firming her resolve. Nothing ventured, nothing gained.

"I'm doing it," she hollered.

"I've got you, Goldie."

If only, she thought with grim purpose, examining a bumpy outcropping that loomed far overhead. That was her goal. From there, the granite sloped upward at an angle that would be easy to climb. She put her right foot on the little bump that had been her previous handhold, wedged her left foot at a slant and used every muscle in her legs to push herself higher. She grunted. There was nothing to grab, it seemed. Her chalked fingertips scratched at unforgiving stone. In desperation, feeling her left foot slipping, she flung herself at the rough surface like a fly at sticky paper and somehow managed to cling long enough to find a new toehold.

"Keep going," Adam urged.

It was either that or fall. She scrambled higher, her thighs burning, her hands on fire, and higher still on a rush of adrenaline when she saw the outcropping was within reach. Latching on to it like a life raft, she dragged her agonized body atop it and rested there, gasping for breath with her heart hammering at her chest. "Nothing to it," she gasped, struck by how good the sun felt on her face and the wind on her perspiration and especially the solid rock beneath her butt.

The last several yards of her ascent were merely a matter of scurrying up the rock using her hands and knees for balance. She took a deep breath when she stood at the top before threading the nylon rope free of her harness and shouting to Adam to let him know she was unhooked.

He came up without a belayer. It was easy for him, she could tell, but still she was biting her tongue between her teeth as he made quick work of it, accomplishing in a couple minutes what had seemed to take her a lifetime. Because of his previous hesitation, she'd been prepared to see him struggle to regain his facility. But not to worry.

"Hey," he said, stepping easily over the edge to the summit. "Congratulations. You made your first climb."

Her heart gave an extra-hard wallop. The man was made for sunshine. It banished the dark shadows in his eyes and lit up his face, his smile, so that it was easy for her to fool herself into believing they were okay as friends. Which they were, they truly were. Okay as friends.

But potentially outstanding as lovers.

"Thanks," she said, collapsing without looking where she was sitting. Any horizontal surface would do for the moment.

Adam crouched beside her and reached out to squeeze her leg in reassurance. He hesitated, then awkwardly patted her kneecap. They'd been like that all morning, jerky and awkward about touching each other as he buckled her into the safety equipment, demonstrated various handholds and weight shifts and stayed close beside her during her first awkward maneuvers over the rocks. "How do you feel?"

She spat grit from her tongue. "Ugh. Let's see. My knees hurt, my elbows hurt, my muscles ache, my fingertips are scraped raw and my insides are like jelly."

"Yet you feel great."

She reflected while unbuckling her helmet. Beneath it, her hair was matted with sweat. "Yeah, I guess I do. Imagine that." She dusted off her jeans. "It's probably just because I'm grateful to be alive."

"Mm."

"I know, I know. You're laughing at me. You're thinking the climb I just did was the equivalent of the bunny slope." She wagged a finger at him. "Let me enjoy my delusions of greatness."

He stood and walked a few feet away before looking at her. He had promised her she could walk down. He knelt and began pulling their rope through the anchor. "You did very well for a beginner."

She surveyed the countryside from her lofty perch, head held high. They were deep into autumn, but at least for today winter seemed far away. There was a mellow warmth in the parched gold of the rustling grasses and dried leaves. The two-lane highway that was Quimby's main road curved around the base of the hill they'd climbed, disappearing into the conifer forests that fringed the town like hula skirts.

"There might be something to this rock-climbing business," she observed. "A method to your madness."

"It's a sport. Nothing more."

"Let's not go that far. I've seen the photos of you climbing in the Himalayas. Sheer madness."

"It's not as risky as it looks. Not when you know what you're doing and take all precautions."

"If it was truly cautious, you wouldn't be interested."

Adam picked up the coiled rope and stood on the edge of the rock, scanning the horizon. "You think I have a death wish?"

"I don't know you well enough to say." She swallowed. "You tell me."

"I do not have a death wish."

"Good." She waited. "But do you have a life wish?"

"What's that?"

"I'm asking you about the future. Or do you intend to

become some wise old man of the mountain, drinking yak milk in a hut on Annapurna?"

He smiled, his eyes distant. "There's an idea. Yak milk's not bad."

She sighed. "You're impossible."

"So I've been told."

"You talk in circles."

"The circle of life is infinite."

Julia shook her head, lapsing into silence because her thoughts were twisted into a knot too snarled to follow. Trying to understand Adam did that to her. He came and sat near her. Together they watched clouds throw shadows across the fallow field. The grass moved like the sea, going from umber to flaxen as the sun chased shadows across the ripples.

She shaded her eyes and looked sideways at Adam. "I believe I'm getting my second breath. Do we have time to make another climb?" Call her a glutton for punishment, but she didn't want the morning to end.

"You've had enough for today. But tomorrow we can head up toward the quarry pond. There are some good rocks around there. Or we can try the Thornhill cliffs."

"I've been up the path there. That was steep and scary enough for me, thank you very much."

"I wouldn't let you attempt a climb beyond your skill level."

She grinned. "You mean I have a skill level?"

He grinned back. "Sort of."

"If you think I can do it..."

"It's more important that you think so."

She saluted. "Absolutely. I am the rock."

"What?"

"It's the Zen chant I made up during my perilous ascent. I respect the rock, I feel the rock, I am the rock." She caressed the sunbaked granite beneath her, certain that she'd never look at a stone the same way again. Which reminded her…

"What are you doing now?" Adam asked when she started crawling with her nose to the stone.

"Looking for something." Not just any rock would do. It had to be a significant rock. She ended up bumping down the side on her rear end and hanging over the outcropping to fish for one of the rocks that were embedded in the crack, working them with her sore fingertips till one came loose. It was quite small, more of a pebble, really, but nicely shaped and striped red and white. She climbed up and gave it to Adam. He looked mystified.

"A replacement rock," she explained. "For the one I lost."

His gaze shifted from her face. "You did the climb. You should keep it," he said, his voice raw as he shoved it abruptly into her hand. He turned away and made a production out of clinking the carabiners and recoiling the ropes.

Julia blanched. She couldn't help it; she was hurt. He didn't want her rock and he didn't want her. Maybe she was missing something in his reasoning, but for the moment she couldn't be rational about what was happening between them. Because she was hurting. Aching.

Ten years of rejection—even rejection cloaked as indifference—was a lot to bear up under.

She swung her arm overhead, meaning to throw the

small rock over the side, but her fingers clenched at the last moment.

Keep it.

For suddenly it had occurred to her that Adam was not indifferent.

Not lately.

There is hope, she thought. *Keep the stone.* When all was said and done, even a dinky little pebble might turn out to be significant.

4

THE WRONG BROTHER, Julia repeated, crushing the note in her hand. Becoming aware of Adam's gaze—and the tingle it caused to run through her—she wrapped the silk robe tightly around herself, rattled that he was seeing her dressed this way, waiting to seduce his brother with such an obvious and conventional setup. Adam would think she was banal. He'd probably laugh at her behind her back.

He would not, she contradicted herself, catching sight of his intent face. Adam's humor was wry and sarcastic, but he wasn't mean. If she asked him to keep quiet, he would.

She collapsed on the bed beside him. "I feel so stupid."

He shifted away from her. Then reached over to awkwardly pat her hand. "Uh, that's okay. It was a mistake. I can go find Zack, if you want."

"No!"

"No?" Adam repeated, meaning, Why not?

"It's too late. This was a dumb idea, anyway. I shouldn't have tried to schedule my—" She stopped, suddenly too aware of the heat of Adam's body and the reaction inside herself, enticing her to lean a little closer, to lower her voice, to touch him, smooth the hair off his forehead....

Oh, no. Absolutely not. She was too smart to give in to her illogical attraction to Adam, who was wild, daring and extremely hazardous to her heart.

Who was, in fact, everything she, and Zack, were not.

No, no, no. Adam was definitely the wrong brother.

BY WEDNESDAY, Julia hadn't yet managed to wrangle Adam into another rock-climbing lesson, even though he'd promised they would go. So she carried on with her professional life as if the personal side wasn't topsy-turvy, answering phones, showing houses, coaxing an older couple out of their seller's remorse and a newlywed couple into the realm of affordability, writing listings that made a fixer-upper bungalow with no southern light sound like a cozy enchanted cottage in the forest. She went out to Evergreen Point several times, but there was never a hint that Adam had stayed there. She wasn't sure he'd need to, since the Brody houseguests had left town. Except for—this according to Gwen at the post office, who always had her finger on Quimby's pulse—one elderly aunt who apparently preferred the Brody hospitality to wheelchair aerobics at the retirement home.

Thursday afternoon, Julia drove to her parents' place for the usual lunchtime visit. The Knoxes owned a junk shop that masqueraded as an antique emporium. It was a big old barn stuffed to the rafters with three decades of flea-market and yard-sale purchases—items like fleets of mismatched ladder-back chairs, apple baskets, old drive-in signs, rusty claw-foot bathtubs and every dented tin watering can, cookie jar and copper Jell-O mold west of the Hudson.

"Julie, Julie, Julie," said her father as he always did, opening his arms for a hug.

"Honey bunny, I have something for your house," said her mother as she always did. The something would turn out to be a butter churn or a plaster cupid, and Julia would have to think of a polite way to turn it down.

Benny and Bonnie Knox were both short, rotund and cheerful. Julia was the apple of their eye—she had a laminated wooden plaque that said so. They thought she was too restrained and orderly, and she thought them too colorful and chaotic, but beneath the exasperation with each other was a lot of love and slightly baffled mutual respect.

"I have no idea what that is, Mom," Julia said with her arm wound around her father's shoulders. He wore six colors and patterns, rubber gloves and a Roast My Nuts barbecue apron that doubled as protective furniture-refinishing gear.

"It's a tea cozy," Bonnie said, modeling the quilted wad as a hat. "Blue and white, you notice, sweetheart? It'll match your dishes. I know how you like things to match."

"Oh, well..." Julia plucked the cozy off her mother's head. A tag dangled from one of the ruffles. Twenty-five cents. "Thanks a lot."

"You want it?" The shock was so great Bonnie nearly stumbled backward into a rack of souvenir spoons.

"I can use a tea cozy," Julia said, thinking of Adam. He never drank coffee—only tea.

"Goodness gracious." Her mother spun in a circle, scanning the shelves of the mismatched-china section of the emporium. "We have teapots galore. A few without chipped spouts, even. Cups! And saucers! And those cunning little silver thingies that you place over the cup to strain the tea—"

"That's quite all right, Mom. I already have a tea set

with plenty of pieces, all handles intact.'' As a child, Julia had been dragged to innumerable kitschy yard sales. In response, she'd vowed to live in a new house where clutter was kept to a minimum. But blood did tell, and she still liked the occasional Sunday-afternoon auction. She even collected blue-and-white china, so she hadn't entirely escaped the Benny and Bonnie Knox ''less isn't more, junk is more'' influence.

Bonnie clucked, casting a nudge of a glance at her husband. ''Better a broken handle than a broken leg. Isn't that right, Benny?''

He scowled at Julia, but the attempt to be stern failed because the man looked like a garden gnome. ''What's this I hear about you taking up rock climbing, my dear?''

Julia tried to explain her motivations. ''It's not like I'm going to climb Everest,'' she concluded. Her parents remained skeptical. They'd always been flummoxed by her athletic abilities, giggling over the possibility that she'd been switched at birth and their real daughter was off somewhere panting to keep up with a family of skiers or tennis players.

''It's that Adam fellow's influence,'' Benny said. ''He's a wild one.''

''Honey bunny, I cringe to think of you dangling over a cliff on only a rope.''

''Mom, you know me. Would I do anything dangerous?'' Luckily she hadn't mentioned the skydiving to anyone but Adam.

''No, you're a good girl.''

''Never given us a moment of worry.''

Julia felt her smile fading. How pathetic was that?

Fortunately, she was able to turn the discussion to Zack and Cathy's wedding. Benny wandered to the back room where he was in the middle of stripping a rocker. In between assisting a carload of blue hairs in search of the perfectly weathered weather vane, Bonnie and Julia rehashed the wedding party, agreeing that Zack had been lucky to get out of his originally scheduled nuptials to Laurel Barnard. "There's a girl who'd buy antiques strictly for their investment value," Bonnie said, shuddering.

After a lunch that consisted of egg salad sandwiches that tasted faintly of dust and varnish—the Knoxes' taste buds had lost function years ago—she said her goodbyes and left for an appointment, carrying both the tea cozy and a tarnished silver tea strainer her mother had insisted upon giving her.

Eve Brody drove up as Julia slipped behind the wheel of her nicely appointed Lincoln Town Car, a staid choice but a necessity for carting around clients.

"Julia!" Eve waved. "Hello!"

Julia rolled down her window. "Hi, Mrs. Brody."

Adam's tall, slender mother stepped out of her car, dressed in a casual but smart sweater and skirt with low-heeled boots and matching purse, her silvered hair swinging around a pair of beaded hoop earrings. She reached into her back seat and pulled out a thick sheaf of pamphlets. "I'm dropping off flyers all over town. Can you take a bunch for your office?"

"Sure." They talked briefly about Mrs. Brody's plan to whip the town into shape, though Julia's mind was not on the current crisis at the water treatment plant. She'd always wanted to be Eve Brody when she grew up, which was probably a large part of why she'd stuck with Zack for so long. As much as she loved her own mother, a muddled, fly-by-the-seat-of-your-pants lifestyle wasn't for her. Eve Brody was so hip and pulled together. She radiated class.

"You must come to dinner, Julia. We miss you at the Brody household."

"Um..."

"Is it too awkward? Why don't you come while Zack is still off on his honeymoon?"

"Not awkward at all, Mrs. Brody." Julia had allowed others to pity her for the loss of Zack because it suited her touchy situation with Adam. That did not mean it wasn't aggravating to be thought of as one of Heartbreak's dejected exes. "You know that Zack and I have remained friends."

Eve swept a swath of hair behind one ear and bent to smile into Julia's car. "Then I'll expect you. Friday night? Sevenish?"

Boxed in. "That would be super, Mrs. Brody."

"Call me Eve." She reached inside and laid a smooth, manicured hand over Julia's, clenched on the steering wheel. "After all, I was almost your mother-in-law."

Julia swallowed. "I'll try."

Eve squeezed and withdrew. "We'll try to rope Adam into a dining chair, as well. Though I suppose you two are seeing plenty of each other as it is?"

Julia shrugged quizzically.

"The rock-climbing lessons? Every day?"

"Every day?"

"You're courageous, I must say. And I'm so grateful that the lessons have given Adam a purpose again. Not to mention a reason to stay in town a while longer. Reuben and I owe you one for that."

"Yes," Julia said.

Eve waved as she moved toward the junk shop. "Tell Adam about dinner when you see him later on." She gestured. "Thornhill cliffs? You must be an excellent student to have advanced so quickly, Julia. I'm terribly impressed!"

AT FIRST Julia wanted to race off to confront Adam about using her as a decoy, but she didn't know where he was and was too conscientious to cancel her appointment for a wild-goose chase. It sounded as though Adam had told his mother they were climbing this afternoon. By the time she finished with her clients, went home to change into jeans and a casual knit shirt, then drove bumpety-bump over the backwoods road that brought her to the cliffs, her reproach had downgraded to a sense of gnawing disappointment. She'd thought they'd grown closer, at least as friends.

November had arrived, and with it a chill in the air. She got out of the car with her jacket slung over her shoulders and stood shivering as she stared at the bleak, gray-thicketed hillside. A dirt trail led twistingly upward through the bush. A half mile of vertical hiking would bring her to the summit. It was the geography on the opposite side of the hill that interested Adam. There the terrain was split into a series of sheer rock walls. He'd been climbing the Thornhill cliffs since he was fifteen, but that didn't make it safe. Especially if he was on his own.

And not operating at one hundred percent.

Don't think that way, Julia told herself as cold needles of fear slipped under her skin. *Stay mad instead. He's perfectly fine. He's blown you off, that's all.*

Adam's Jeep was parked by the side of the road. A glance in the back confirmed that much of his climbing equipment was gone. He'd stressed to her that she must always climb with a partner. It was doubtful whether he followed the rule himself, being the solitary cuss that he was.

Fear prickled in her bloodstream.

She took off at a jog. The trail soon grew steep, and she had to slow down, clutching at bare branches here and there in her scramble up the hillside. Some of them broke, and she whipped the pieces away in exasperation. At the halfway mark, she was forced to stop and catch her breath, her heart pounding. A few hardy birds warbled in the barren trees, making a mockery of her growing dread.

She got going again, her mind keeping pace with her feet. Adam could take care of himself—he'd been doing it for years and years, through radical adventures that would make the average person book a lifetime seat in an easy chair. He was too damned independent to ever question himself.

Or he had been—before the accident. Before Laurel Barnard.

Adam's affair with Laurel had been a shock to Julia. While she'd adjusted to the idea of losing him to an ongoing infatuation with the great outdoors, seeing him with Laurel was a major kick in the ego, especially since she'd always tried to tell herself it wasn't *her* he'd run from, it was the thought of any commitment at all.

Learning otherwise had put her rationalizations—and her emotions—into a tailspin.

She wasn't entirely clear on the sequence of events, but she knew that on one of Adam's trips home, Laurel had turned all the beauty, charm and seductive skills she usually lavished on Zack—to little avail—toward his younger brother instead. Adam, less sophisticated about womanly wiles than Zack, was ensnared. And Julia was devastated, especially when it seemed Adam was getting serious about Laurel.

Then suddenly he'd left town without notice, and a few weeks later Laurel was announcing her engagement to Zack. Quimby had swirled with rumors. None of them had seemed logical at the time, though Julia's suspicion was that Laurel had used Adam as a dupe. Julia had hurt for him almost as much as she hurt for herself—even more, after she'd learned about his car wreck. Only her acquaintance with Adam's stubborn pride had stopped her from racing to his bedside. She knew he wouldn't want her there—another bitter pill to swallow. The ensuing months and slow trickle of news about his status and long recovery had been agonizing.

Which was when she'd realized she had to stop waiting for her life to begin and start living it.

With or without Adam, she'd decided.

Please, please, God. Not without. I want him by my side. I always have.

The sky was a cloudless cobalt. Unresponsive. The trees and spiky brush had grown sparse. Uncomforting.

The stark truth hit her—what she'd always known but hadn't let herself state clearly.

Adam Brody is the love of my life.

The crest was near, just beyond a steep slurry of rocks and gravel. Julia's lungs felt as though they were tearing open, but she pushed harder, skidding in the slippery gravel, her cheeks damp with tears and sweat. She had no real reason to think that Adam was in trouble. Her sense of foreboding could just as easily be a figment of her churning imagination.

She was never like this. Never out of control, her pulse a primal drumbeat pounding at her skull.

"Adam!" His name had burst from her like a gunshot. She slammed to a stop.

He was sitting on the edge of the cliff. Unharmed. Intact. Unmoving?

"Adam—my God, I thought—" She went to him, stumbling in her relief, dropping to her knees behind him. Her hug was hard enough to crack his ribs. "Oh, Adam..."

"Get off me," he snapped, knocking her away as he scrambled to his feet. The movement was too abrupt, and his knee buckled. She gasped. He was on the very edge of the cliff. One misstep and he might go over the side.

He shook his head and shoulders angrily and regained his balance, walking casually along the edge as if he were on a Sunday stroll. But she'd seen his pallor and the strain etched in lines upon his face. Something had happened.

She was on her rump, gravel biting into her palms. The overlook stretched before her, silent and empty as only a colorless November landscape could be. Exactly the kind of open space and freedom Adam loved. There was no anchor or topline to be seen. That meant he'd been lead climbing, attaching the rope to the rock as he ascended. Far more dangerous. His equipment was strewn nearby, the rope abandoned in a snarled mess, the harness positioned as if it had been ripped off his body and flung away. There were patches of dirt on his long-sleeved shirt and pants. His hands were scraped raw beneath a filmy layer of chalk dust.

Her mouth was coppery with dread. *What had happened?*

He kept his back to her. As she walked to him, his shoulders rose and fell with a deep breath. "Adam?" She put out a tentative hand. It trembled visibly, and she snatched it back. "You've been climbing?" *On your own.*

"A test," he said. "That's all."

Again, her hand hovered in midair. So much tension radiated off him, she didn't quite dare touch.

"I failed," he said acidly, and moved farther away, sending a few pebbles bouncing over the edge into the trees far below.

Solo, she thought, trying not to imagine what might have occurred. She didn't want to know. Didn't want another picture of him in danger, struggling, maybe hurt, finding a place in her head.

Too late. It was there.

Clearly, he didn't want comfort. She turned and walked jerkily to the climbing gear and crouched there, hoping he wouldn't see how shaky her hands were as she arranged the nylon rope and lengths of webbing into neat piles. "You told me never to solo," she said after a while, when the silence became too heavy. She couldn't pretend she hadn't been scared out of her wits.

He didn't respond at once. She closed her eyes tight and swallowed again and again, counting each second.

Finally he said, mockingly, "I'm experienced."

"But you're coming off an injury!"

"Don't worry. I survived in one piece." He worked his shoulder, loosening stiff muscles. "One damaged piece," he added bitterly, under his breath.

Her heart twisted at the words, but outwardly she ignored them. He wouldn't want her sympathy any more than he'd wanted the physical comfort she'd offered. He was a solitary man, accustomed to denial and deprivation. How very sad, she thought, ducking her chin to hide the tears that welled in her eyes.

Silently she cursed herself for insisting on the rock-climbing lessons. Adam might not have come here if she hadn't coaxed him into it. In her heart she knew that he'd tested himself alone because he didn't want to fail in front of her.

"It's not your fault," he said, suddenly standing beside her.

She glanced up, then away, dashing at the moisture making her vision glimmer.

"I'm sorry, Julia." He crouched next to her, and for the first time she saw the raw red scrape on his forehead. Her stomach squeezed into a knot as she battled to hold back the desire to touch him, hold him, kiss him...comfort him.

"Sorry for climbing solo?"

His eyes had darkened to a dreary green, like a pine in winter. Brittle with cold. She wanted to grab him by the shoulders and shake some lowly human emotion and neediness into him.

Who are you to complain, Miss Always in Control?

"No. Sorry I pushed you away," he said. "Did I hurt you?"

She shook her head. "Not this time."

"What?"

Her eyes opened wide. "I didn't mean that."

He dragged a dirty hand through his hair, regarding her warily. "When did I hurt you?"

She thrust the harness at him, then the rope and the metal climbing aids. "Nothing. Never mind. Here, take these."

He let the gear drop and grabbed her by the arms instead, pulling them both to their feet. "I wouldn't hurt you. I wouldn't hurt anyone—"

She wrenched herself away. "Not physically," she said, pouring all her emotions into her burning, blazing eyes. "But how do you think we feel when you're out here—out there—" she waved at the open air "—risking your goddamn life!"

"It's not your concern."

"You can't just tell someone not to care." The way he had ten years ago, she realized. He'd felt guilty and ashamed and he'd thought they could turn back the clock and act as if nothing had happened between them. He'd thought she would stop loving him if he stayed away.

Maybe she'd thought so, too.

But it hadn't worked that way. She loved him still. Her run up the mountain had stripped away all pretenses in that regard.

"This was a mistake," Adam said.

"You bet it was!"

"Your lessons," he explained.

"No. Your foolish bravado."

His eyes narrowed. At their corners, ground-in dirt created crow's-feet of bisecting lines.

"I don't know what happened here today, Adam, but you've got to face it. At least for a while, you shouldn't be climbing alone—"

"Then I won't climb," he said through clenched teeth.

"You're going to give it up?" She didn't believe it for a second, despite the desperate promises he'd told her he'd made after the accident. "I don't think so. Besides, we made a bargain. Since you've been using the house—" she was taking a shot in the dark there "—I expect to be repaid. Tomorrow we'll have another session. And after that, another. We can work ourselves into shape together." She put her fists on her hips, daring him to object. "Else I'm turning you in to your parents. And Zack."

That made him smile, if wryly. He shrugged as if it didn't matter. But she'd seen the look in his eyes—respect.

She thrust her chin at him. "What do you say?"

"Sounds like a plan," he conceded.

Full of bluster, she strode up to him and stuck out her hand.

They shook on it.

"YOUR MOTHER invited me for dinner Friday night," Julia murmured, hovering over Adam with a swatch of gauze soaked in antiseptic. The plump cushion of one of her overstuffed armchairs felt nice and cushy beneath his neck. Comfortable. Easy on his aching muscles. He wanted to close his eyes and let Julia's soothing touch and calm, clean house whirl him away into a pleasant daze.

The sting of the cleanser woke him up. Weakness, he thought. He was riddled with it.

"Will Zack and Cathy be back by then?" she asked, blowing softly on his scrape.

His eyelids drifted shut. "Don't think so."

"I won't come if it's too uncomfortable...."

"Uncomfortable for whom?"

"Right." She slapped a bandage onto his forehead. "Why should it be uncomfortable? You and I are only buddies."

"You were their maid of honor."

Julia sat on the arm of the chair, frowning over the first-aid kit as she packed it up and set it aside. "I wasn't talking about Zack and Cathy. I'm not uncomfortable around them. It's you who—" She rolled her gaze to the ceiling, exhaling noisily. "Sheesh, Adam, you're so obtuse."

"Does that mean you don't want to be buddies?" His voice came out soft and lazy—unguarded. Somewhere at the back of his mind he knew this was heedless, but he couldn't make himself care.

His fingers slid along her arm, pushing up the sleeve of her soft knitted shirt. She caught her breath, her skin prickling beneath his touch.

"You do." She slumped, moving a little closer. "Want to be buddies. Only buddies. Isn't that what you said?"

"It was you who said it."

Her skin was warm now. She was warm. Like the sun. He closed his eyes and breathed deeply, recognizing that Julia had always been like the sun to him—golden, life-giving warmth. Why shouldn't he bask in her presence, let some of her beguiling contentment sink into his cold bones?

He found her hand, dragged it slowly across his chest. She tilted above him, halfway in his lap until she braced herself on the chair's opposite arm. Somewhere in the sparse, clean living room a clock ticked, making him think of all the minutes and hours and days he'd purposely spent away from Julia...when she was what he searched for.

The sun, the glorious sun.

Her face filled his field of vision, flushed to a peachy glow, smooth amber hair swinging forward against her cheeks. Her eyes were huge. Her lips were parted, trembling slightly. He reached for her, mere inches that seemed like miles until finally he cupped her face in his hands and she made a soft, low sound filled with pleasure, like the humming of honeybees, drawing it out until the air around them vibrated with it. He felt her breath on his lips, smelled the delicate female scent of her skin mingled with a pungent earthiness.

Kiss her. *Kiss her.*

"No," he groaned, even as he drew her to his mouth. "This is wrong."

A startled expression flashed across her face. She got her arms between them and pushed on his shoulders, levering herself away. Cool air swooshed into the place where she had been, and he shuddered, reviling the emptiness.

Julia backed away. "Wait," he said, rising partway from the chair, his sore muscles protesting.

"I don't want to be your mistake." She turned toward the wall of windows, holding up a hand to keep him at bay. "I went through that before. It wasn't very pleasant." Her shoulders hunched, and she pressed her knuckles to her midriff, emitting a mirthless laugh. "I'm feeling kind of sick, so do you think you could leave now?"

"Let me explain."

"You wouldn't let me explain ten years ago."

He winced. "Oh, that."

"Yes. Unlike you, I haven't forgotten what happened in that motel room." She clutched her ribs. "There's nothing quite as memorable as being an eighteen-year-old ex-virgin who's just been told by the boy she made love with for the first time that he thinks it was all a stupid, regrettable mistake."

Adam couldn't answer. Denials or excuses would ring hollow. They'd avoided the subject for so long he'd begun to believe she'd forgotten it. It was easier that way to forget it himself. Or at least pretend to.

"Yeah," Julia said miserably, shooting him quick, darting glances. "There it is. The big bad monster emerges from the closet. We screwed things up—literally—and nothing's ever been the same since."

"How could it be? You were Zack's girlfriend." The same old refrain, hammering at the inside of his skull. Her anguish tore at him. He'd caused it. It didn't matter that he'd been only eighteen himself and too brash to stop and evaluate the ramifications. The truth was he'd taken his guilt and shame and run far away, leaving her to the day-to-day strain of facing up to Zack. A terrible fate. Why hadn't he seen it?

"Zack and I were perfect together," Julia mused, staring off into the ravine outside her windows. "Everyone said so." She smiled sadly. "Of course, they didn't know about me and you."

Adam's muscles cramped. Wavering on his feet, he clenched his fists, keeping his balance through sheer will.

"Me and you." She looked him up and down, her eyes remote. "The big mistake. So very imperfect..."

But so powerful. Strong enough, he thought, to last all these years.

She waved at him. "Go away. It's all right. We're just buddies now."

No, they weren't. He'd known they couldn't be right from the start, when she'd walked up to him at the reception with her absurd request. If only he'd put a penny in the bank and listened to his common "cents."

Adam took a step toward Julia, then stopped as the familiar tightness in his lower back seeped lower, turning his left leg numb and useless.

She had flinched at the sound of his footstep. "Go," she said again, not looking at him. "Go away."

Her fragility was gut-wrenching. And he was too paralyzed by his own weaknesses to offer comfort. Damn his pride, but he couldn't let her see him lurching around, making stumbling, bumbling attempts to soothe her. Without the cane, he might even fall. And then she'd have to put aside her despair and help him instead of hate him. She would pity him. Or worse, act like it didn't matter that he'd returned to Quimby only because he was nursing his wounds like a wounded bear crawling home to its den.

Cursing inside, he moved slowly and carefully toward the stairs. They looked as treacherous as any mountain he'd ever scaled, but he would grit his teeth and get up them even if he had to drag his leg behind him like a ball and chain.

Owing to rash immaturity, he'd been half a man when he left Julia the first time.

He was leaving her again, and nothing much had changed.

But it would, he swore to himself. *This time, it would.*

JULIA STAYED at the windows even after Adam finally left. His slow climb up the stairs had melted away the last shreds of her anger toward him, but she hadn't let herself go to help him. Not this time.

She'd wanted his kiss so badly she could still feel it on her lips—the tingling proximity, the desire that had filled her like honey in a jug. One tip and it would have spilled over them, trapping them in its sticky sweetness until their satisfaction had washed it all away.

And what then?

Probably Adam had been right to hesitate. They were headed for heartache—or, at least, she was. She had no clue about his thoughts on the subject since he'd said so very little. Except that he still considered her a mistake.

Cuts like a knife.

"Enough," she said, turning to stare at the empty room. She'd created a haven of peace and quiet for herself, with walls painted in wide stripes of cream and ice blue. The floors were bare wood, clean and shining, the furnishings few—two plump armchairs with white denim slipcovers, a love seat in steel blue. Sheer, floaty curtains the color of the winter sky. A grandfather clock. A plain table. A lamp.

Clean and pure and untouched, she thought.

"Don't be so dramatic." She had a good life—a career and friends and outside interests. The only element she'd been waiting on was Adam Brody, and if another suitable man had shown up, she'd have married him without making a last-ditch effort for Adam, wouldn't she? Wouldn't she?

Probably. Maybe.

Maybe not.

She pressed her palms to her forehead. She needed a shower. She needed to feel clean again.

Her eyes cut to the chair as she walked out of the room. A smudge of brown dirt marked the place where Adam had rested his head.

ADAM SAT in his Jeep outside the Brody house, holding the cane in his lap. He didn't want to use it; his mother would fret if she saw him with it. *To use it would take more courage than not to,* he told himself. *It's a different kind of strength.*

Or weakness.

Julia had been right about him climbing the Thornhill cliffs without a partner. It had been foolhardy. He used to solo there all the time; he'd known the various paths up the rocks, each crevasse and handhold, as well as he knew the back of his hand. The terrain was still familiar—his body was not.

The climb had been tougher than he'd anticipated. By the time he'd reached the Smoker, a vertical indent cut into the rock face, he'd already been exhausted. With his weakened back protesting all the way, the Smoker had been a bitch to climb—it demanded techniques he hadn't used in a year and a half. Partway up it, his left leg had weakened, and he'd fallen down the narrow chimney, banging and scraping against the rock until the safety line caught with a snap, stopping his descent. It had taken him many long minutes to climb back up the Smoker, a section of the climb that he used to do with ease.

But he'd do better next time.

If Julia was still game.

No reason for her to be, after he'd treated her so shabbily. He regretted his rough dismissal on the hilltop—that had come out of his frustration. But he couldn't take back his other words, because he believed them. Kissing Julia was wrong. It was dishonorable. Plain and simple. No equivocation.

He should leave town. Now.

Then she'll always think of you as half a man.

Adam nodded. He had to prove himself to her. Not by leaving—by staying. And doing the right thing.

He set the cane on the street and stepped out of the Jeep. His muscles were still protesting the abuse, but the contractions had ceased. A long, hot bath would help. He thought of his small closet of a bathroom upstairs, then of the whirlpool tub in Julia's show house. A bargain was a bargain.

5

"JULIA?" ADAM SAID, very softly.

She hitched her breath and turned to face him, shivering inside and trying not to show it even though the battle had probably been lost the moment she'd opened the door. Previously, there had been moments she'd suspected Adam had guessed how she felt about him. Now, though, the attraction was unmistakable. Reciprocal. The air buzzed with it.

But he was a risk. A dangerous risk.

"Goldie?" he said, and she was lost. She'd always loved the way he called her Goldie, as if she were a rare treasure to him.

She understood that her plan to present herself to Zack for devirginization was a last-ditch attempt to save herself from her barely controllable desire for Adam. The crazy recklessness of choosing the wild brother instead of the good one was such an overwhelming option she'd retreated to the safety of her relationship with Zack.

But destiny had intervened.

Julia surrendered to it. "Oh, Adam. I'm so glad you're here." She closed her eyes, willing him to kiss her.

"THREE BEDROOMS, each with a private bath," Julia said by rote. "The office on the ground floor can easily be converted to a fourth bedroom, as needed. There's a three-quarter powder room here, just off the foyer."

The clients poked their heads inside, oohing over the Kohler spigots.

"Shall we go upstairs?" Julia prompted, eager to get the tour finished. Her nerve endings felt all skittery.

"I want another look at the kitchen," the wife said. "Harold? What did you think of the tile—will it match my pot holders and carpets?"

"I'll give you a moment." Julia smiled dutifully as the middle-aged couple went to the kitchen for the second time, despite her explanation that they could select their own finishing details if they chose one of the houses under construction. Some people had no imagination.

And some had too much. Julia didn't know why—there was no sign of Adam in the clean, spacious rooms—but she felt his presence, and it was making her as nervous as a cat in a haunted house. She wasn't sure what to say to him. Definitely not *I've always loved you.*

When Harold and Ivy Strohmeyer returned, she herded them up the stairway. She'd already checked the house to be certain it was ready to show, and there'd been no sign of disturbance except for a towel askew in the master bath. Which she might have done herself, brushing against it. So there was no need for skittishness.

After her spiel, she left the clients to wander around the bedrooms by themselves and went up the spiral staircase to the cupola. Built-in benches encircled the windowed octagon, fitted with tufted cushions and pillows. It was a marvelous lookout point, perfect for a few quiet moments with a book and a cup of tea, watching the lake glimmer like a sapphire through the tree branches.

Her nose wrinkled. "Bell jar. Huh."

Activity in the development drew her gaze from the lake. Landscapers worked at one of the finished homes, rolling out big wheels of sod. At another, the sounds of construction—whining saws and hammer blows—filled the air. Julia's gaze drifted toward the house across the way, where she and Adam had stood together in the open cupola only a few weeks ago. It looked very different now, solid with wood and glass. Men crawled over the house like busy little ants, applying siding and shingles.

One figure, crouching at the edge of the roof, caught her eye. "*Adam?*" She mouthed the word.

She squinted. Could it be? A knotted bandanna covered the top of the roofer's bowed head. At first she was doubtful, but then the man moved, and she was certain. No one but Adam moved like that—lithe and agile as a cat, even after his injuries.

He wore jeans and a sweatshirt and heavy boots. A carpenter's belt was slung around his waist. He heaved a bundle of shingles up the slope of the roof, knelt and began nailing them in place with an electric nail gun.

Adam. Working construction. Well, why not? He must know the limits of his strength.

Or he wanted to test those limits, she thought, remembering him sitting dejectedly on the ledge of the Thornhill cliffs. She definitely shouldn't scurry over to cluck at him like a mother hen.

Julia shepherded the Strohmeyers outside and walked them along the curved street, past the vehicles parked at angles half on and half off the pavement. "Would you like to peek inside one of the houses under construction? This one is almost finished." She picked up yellow hard hats from the foreman, who agreed to take charge and escort the couple inside for a five-minute tour.

Julia jogged around the corner, tipping back her helmet as she scanned the roofline. There he was. "Adam Brody!" she called. "Imagine meeting you here."

Adam rose and walked to the edge of the roof. He peeled gloves off his hands and stood flexing his fingers while he looked at her. His expression was cautious. "Hey, Goldie."

She relaxed a degree. "How did this happen?"

"I needed a job." He walked casually to the ladder and climbed down, jumping the last few rungs with an easy masculine grace. A puff of dust rose around his boots. He strolled toward her, slapping the gloves together, and she was hit with a wave of keen longing, aware of every inch of him, from the shock of brown hair peeping from beneath the bandanna to the worn seams of the jeans wrapped around his narrow hips and lean, taut thighs. Testosterone was thick in the air, what with all the workmen hustling about, but Adam's heated skin exuded a special brand of musk. The weather was brisk but sunny and warm, and he'd been sweating, perspiration darkening the soft, worn shirt that clung to his chest.

A corresponding warmth trickled into Julia's palms and cheeks. The distraction of it made her forget her discomfort. She thrust her chin out. "Roofing, huh? Can you handle it?"

His brows went up, but his smile was negligent. "Sure."

She waited. No enlightenment was forthcoming. Typical Adam, playing it close to the vest. "How did you come by the job?" she asked, her tone suspicious. "I hope you didn't get caught at the house by the construction crew."

"Nope. I was at the lake the other day and happened to talk to a few of the workers. They told me roofers were needed. So this morning I walked right up to the foreman and asked for a job like a regular Joe."

She wiped her hands on her wool skirt. "You've worked construction before." Zack had mentioned it.

"Yep."

"And what else?" She squinted at him, pondering. "Tree surgeon, wasn't it?" She could picture him, clambering among the treetops like a monkey.

"Yep."

"Weren't you a river guide out in Idaho?" She'd thought that might be the job he'd stick with.

"Hated it," he said. "Too many fat tourists with cameras, thinking they'd ride the river like the Teacups at Disney World."

"That's mean." She had to chuckle, though. "What am I missing from your résumé?"

"I started doing some woodworking this past year, when I wasn't much good for anything else." He shifted from foot to foot. "Did you want references? What's your purpose here, Jule?"

She folded her arms. "Oh, just checking up on you."

His face hardened, the usual mulish independence darkening his eyes as if a shadow had been thrown across the sun. "No need," he said.

"I guess not. You seem to be doing fine." This wasn't at all what she'd meant to talk about.

"Our bargain doesn't make you responsible for me." His voice had softened. She responded to it like a cat to a trouser leg, leaning toward him with every hair on her body bristling in anticipation.

Then she caught herself. They weren't lovers, they were buddies. After ten years, you'd think she could remember that instead of getting all fizzy over the way he wore his jeans.

She sucked in a breath, tilting her head as she looked at him. "Do we still have a bargain?"

"Yeah. Sure."

Just not an understanding.

"Because I was wondering if I should call your mother to cancel dinner."

"You don't have to do that."

"You don't want me to?"

"I'm thinking of my mother." His brows went up and down as he gave her the once-over. "It's not like you to be rude and cancel at the last minute, Julia."

"I was thinking of *you,*" she blurted, holding herself still with an effort. The way he'd looked her over made her want to preen and strut and rub up against him so there was no possible way he could avoid their mutual attraction. "*You're* the one who doesn't want me around." She smiled a little teasingly and took two steps closer. "I'm just worried that your formidable discipline isn't up to snuff these days. Having me around, tempting you, might cause undue stress."

That got him. His brows drew together, his face going

dark as a storm cloud. He looked like he wanted to speak, but she'd captured his tongue.

She advanced till she was right in his face, the space between them a scanty inch. "But since you're all right with it, I will come, after all."

Someone on the rooftop called to Adam to get back to work. He glanced over his shoulder and threw the man a hasty wave, then turned all his well-honed concentration on Julia. She kept her expression guileless, holding her gaze steady on his even when he touched a fingertip—one riveting fingertip—to her chin.

He took the finger away. Cleared his throat. "Yeah, you'll come."

She narrowed her eyes at him, having second thoughts. His tone...

"Dare you," he said.

DINNER WITH the Brodys was a unique affair, at least to Julia, even though she'd done it countless times in the past. She'd loved being invited over during the years she was dating Zack, because the Brodys were so exceedingly normal. Dinner with her family was a catch-as-catch-can deal. Often mealtime would pass without notice. Or there might be a pot of chili or spaghetti on a back burner, not to be confused with a simmering batch of beeswax concocted by her father. If you were lucky, you'd find a clear space at the dining table, which was usually cluttered with the parts and supplies of ongoing repairs. Several times, the table itself couldn't be found—Benny or Bonnie had sold it to one of the antique shoppers they'd let wander around their house. One table—a Biedermeyer knockoff—had been sold out from beneath Julia as she sat with her homework and an after-school snack.

Whereas the Brody house was always the same. The same blue-and-white dining room with a highly polished cherry table and eight matching chairs. Crisp white damask linens, white Spode china with a blue flower pattern around the rim, sparkling crystal and real silver flatware. Reuben Brody sitting at one end, slightly rumpled in a button-down shirt, Eve Brody at the other, her hair upswept and her smile gracious. Adam and Zack across from each other—as different as night and day except for their coloring. Zack was usually fresh from the shower after a game of basketball or a swim, smiling and chatting about his day. As a teenager, Adam had tended to slouch, staring out the window and forgetting to eat, saying nothing about where he'd gone or what he'd done or why he had a new bandage or bruise or rope burn.

But that was ten years ago, Julia reminded herself. Times had changed.

She sat next to Aunt Delilah, who was hard of hearing and kept referring to her as Adam's girl. Julia had given up correcting her, especially since Adam didn't help, only looked at her across the table, lifting a sardonic brow.

He didn't slump and he was freshly showered from his day at the job site, but he still tended to gaze out the window every now and then, tuning out the proceedings.

Julia reached with her foot and tapped him on the ankle under the table. "Your aunt was asking about your new job."

Adam's gaze shifted from the window to her face...and stayed there. "Roofing," he said in the direction of Aunt Delilah, who looked up from her coleslaw in momentary confusion, her fork trembling.

"Eh, what?" she said.

He repeated loudly, "Roofing. That's my job." The elderly woman nodded vaguely and focused on her plate.

"Another temporary seasonal job," Reuben Brody said, shrugging his narrow shoulders. "Isn't it time you thought about a permanent profession? Winter will be here before long, and then you'll be out in the cold, son. Pun intended."

"I'll be gone by then," Adam answered. "All I need is a stash to travel on."

Julia fumbled the knife as she buttered a roll. *No surprise there,* she told herself. *No reason to get all silly and fluttery over the prospect of continuing your conventional little life without Adam. You knew he'd be moving on.*

His mother looked resigned. "Where to this time?"

"Haven't decided." Adam's voice was brooding. Julia sensed his gaze on her, but she didn't look up. "I've got a few feelers out."

"We thought you were staying through the holidays." Eve tilted her head at Julia. "Julia, can't you persuade Adam to stay until Christmas, at least?"

Julia plastered on a blank smile. "Why would he listen to me?"

Aunt Delilah smacked her lips. "Girlies know how to get around their boyfriends."

"To get around Adam I'd have to jump off a mountain."

A distinct silence fell across the table. Julia pressed her lips together. *Oops.* She'd said that out loud, hadn't she? She shoveled in a forkful of mashed potatoes.

Aunt Delilah cackled.

Yes, indeed, she'd said it out loud. As if she was his girlfriend. As if she would do anything to keep him close.

Eve smiled and handed Adam a dish of peas. "It seems that our Julia has got your number."

He scowled. "No one's falling off any mountains."

"Jumping," Julia blurted. "Of my own free will."

His eyes were bright and hard. "Then you'd better make damn well sure you've got a parachute."

She shook her head. No. It was clear to her now. With Adam, you didn't play it cautiously. You didn't hold back, thinking of safety and broken hearts. You shed yourself of encumbrances and leaped into the great unknown.

Which was probably too much to ask of a woman so safety-conscious her premiums alone had paid for her insurance agent's new car.

"Are we talking about persuasion," Adam's father said, "or are we talking about risk? Because I've been thinking, and it seems to me that risk is a game of Russian roulette. Take enough turns, son, and you're bound to blow your head off."

Eve drew in a breath. "What an awful analogy to use, Reuben."

Adam winced. "C'mon, Dad, that's just..."

"I'm keeping an eye on him," Julia announced. "We've been climbing together every day this past week—" she smiled pointedly at him while he flushed with guilt "—and we're being as careful and cautious as little mice, I promise you."

Eve seemed faintly relieved. "But how long will that last?"

"The boy needs to be domesticated," said Aunt Delilah, poking at her plate. "What's the orange goo, eh?"

"Chutney. It's good for you." That was Adam, obviously desperate for distraction.

Reuben nodded. "That's true."

"Vitamin A," said Adam.

"The love of a good woman," said Eve, gazing fondly at Julia.

"That would do wonders," added Reuben, aiming a nod at his son.

"Carrots and squash." Adam stared straight ahead.

Julia thought it was funny. At the same time her heart gave a little kick in her chest. "Don't look at me, Mr. and Mrs. Brody. I'm only learning how to climb rocks. I don't train wild animals."

"It's easy," Eve said, glancing significantly at her husband. Julia was dubious. She couldn't imagine mild, homely, domesticated Reuben Brody as a maverick young buck.

"All a wild thing needs is a few loving applications of persuasion, and it'll come to you of its own free will, gentle as can be," Reuben said, his eyes glinting with a private memory that was obviously shared with his wife. Seeing them look at each other that way gave Julia an odd little twitch of understanding. So that's how it was—Reuben had tamed Eve, not the other way around. Living proof that a conventional life wasn't necessarily a dreaded outcome.

But not, she imagined, for Adam. He didn't take notice any more than he heeded warnings or advice.

"I don't believe in chaining wild animals in the back yard," she said, watching for his reaction. But he was eating the chutney with too much concentration. This was the strangest dinner conversation she'd ever had at the Brodys'. Usually they talked about sports, weather and Quimby politics in an orderly fashion.

"If you love someone, let them wee," Aunt Delilah announced, looking more alert. "Sting," she added. "Not so peppy for wheelchair aerobics as Britney Spears, but the young man has a philosophy to sing to."

Julia sputtered a nervous laugh.

The old lady nodded beside her. "I deejay in the rec room Monday afternoons. It's not drive time—"

"Set them free," Adam said.

"It's nap time," his aunt continued. "They won't let me get jiggly with it. 'Fraid I'll get the oldsters' blood up."

He tried again. "The line is set them free, Aunt Delilah."

"I know that," she said crabbily, flapping a gnarled hand at him. "But we're old. My version works better for the Depends generation."

Julia smiled behind her napkin. Adam conceded with a snort of amusement.

Eve took control in her usual efficient way. "Are we ready for dessert?" she said brightly.

"Bring on the chocolate," Aunt Delilah said. "And lots of it." She nudged Julia with a sharp elbow and said sotto voce, albeit more voce than sotto, "It's a scientific fact. A little chocolate puts the giddy-up into us single gals."

"I'll help clear." Reuben brushed against his wife on the way into the kitchen, and she nearly purred. Thinking they were cute, Julia smiled at the memories that sprang up. Reuben and Eve Brody had always been the very model of a modern marriage: close, affectionate, respectful. Best friends. Equal partners. Everything she'd aspired to.

With Zack.

Yet here she was, her gaze shooting straight to Adam, her heartbeat escalating, her temperature rising...and her expectations dropping with a thud.

Because he, of course, was looking out the window.

JULIA SAT on the white wrought-iron bench alone, her long skirt falling in neat folds around her crossed legs. She wore a pair of low suede boots with an inch of ribbed white sock showing at the ankle. Between the stockings and the flowered skirt was a small expanse of leg. Adam had been looking at that little bit of bare leg for the past five minutes. His powers of concentration were formidable, but staring at a leg—even Julia's leg—was nonsensical.

Boy, did he have a problem.

"We have a problem," Julia said without turning her head. Of course she knew he was there, sitting on the ground beneath one of the graceful weeping willows that lined the riverbank, sheltered by its arch of bare branches like a bird in a cage. She'd known it from the time she'd wandered out of the house, around the dead brown garden and to the bench—all without looking directly at him. Very subtle, he thought. Apparently she was taking this taming-the-wild-animal stuff to heart.

"We have a problem and I think we should talk about it." She turned her face slightly in his direction so he saw the bold lines of her profile, softened by an arc of cheek and the sweep of her lowered lashes. She had a strong face and a forthright manner. Her decisions were usually quick and clean. "Get it all out in the open," she said, flicking her hair from her face. He'd always been drawn by her fighting spirit, knowing it was tempered by kindness and generosity.

She was as admirable a person as Zack.

The idea that she might possibly prefer the second-place brother, that their one time together was more than a horrific mix-up, was staggering.

"Especially since we're going to be climbing together," she concluded.

The yellowed leaves of the willow crunched underfoot as he parted the sweep of branches and went to join her on the bench. His parents used to come out here in the warm summer evenings to get away from the noise of two battling brothers in the house. They'd held hands. Sometimes talked, usually not. He'd look out the window at them before going to bed, relishing, without realizing it, the security of their family and his position in it. Even after he'd become an adult, he occasionally brought up the image of his parents sitting together, side by side. Especially when he was far from home and cut off too long from human contact.

Julia stole a quick look at him from the corner of her eyes before casually lacing her fingers around one knee. He cleared his throat. "Silence is golden."

"Yeah, you would say that, Zen master."

He leaned back and stretched out his legs, dropping his arm along the back of the bench. He could have closed his eyes and stayed there with her forever, not talking, just listening to the gentle lapping of the river and the soft rustling of the dried leaves and rushes, enjoying the feel of her beside him.

Julia's booted foot swung, keeping pace with each second of silence. A low thrumming awareness started up inside him—hell, no, it only reasserted itself despite his suppression—licking his veins with fire. He always wanted her. It was a visceral thing, a constant. He was just very good at denying himself the pleasure of indulging in either memories of what they'd had or fantasies of what it would be like to have it again.

His silence prompted her sound of frustration. "Talk about being the rock. You've got it down pat."

"Who, me?" he said. Julia's chin had dimpled begrudgingly—it was the only habitual facial gesture she had that was less than serene. But endearing. Seeing it made the heat inside him burst into flame.

On his other visits home, it had been easier keeping his distance. This time the ante was upped considerably because he was spending time with her, getting closer to her, even touching her. He wanted to keep doing it—all of it. He wanted to wrap his arms around her and hold her close while he tasted her warm, sweet lips; he wanted to kiss her in the sunshine with the wind in her hair and laughter in her eyes; he wanted to lay with her at night beneath a diamond-laden sky, their naked bodies moving together in primal rhythms as old as nature itself.

"The last thing we need is talk." He was angry with himself for being so weak about her. But he couldn't stop his feelings, his base desires. They boiled down deep and surged up with too much force. He couldn't deny them forever, especially now, when they were burning away what he knew to be right. And wrong.

"You're wrong." She held herself poised. "We need—"

Dammit. Julia let out a startled gasp as Adam roughly took her by the shoulders. "All we need is this," he said, his voice harsh in his throat, and then he covered her half-open mouth in an angry, passionate kiss that blasted every hint of conflict and caution out of his head. He wanted her. He'd always wanted her. That was everything he needed to know.

After the first instant of shock, Julia met his embrace with equal force. The kiss was almost brutal, hard and thrusting as they slammed against each other with ten years of pent-up frustration. Her teeth were bared, clashing against his as their tongues mated boldly. He gripped her slender waist tight enough to snap her in two, except that she was as strong and flexible as a green willow, molded against his chest, the fingers of one hand digging into his shoulder, the other clutching a handful of hair at his nape. He felt her breasts, her diamond-point nipples, her heartbeat racing to catch up to his. He felt her savage desperation. Tasted it, even, like hot salty tears rising up the back of his throat.

He was voracious. She was brazen. Together, they were wild, desperate, unapologetic. He lowered his hands to pull her hips closer to the aching ridge of his erection. They slid lower on the bench, almost reclining with her on top, moving against him with inciting little wiggles and thrusts. He groaned, clutching at the flexing curves of her sexy behind. Through her silky skirt, he felt the edge of elastic on her panties. An erotic image burst vividly inside his head. He could rip them away and pin her to the ground and sink himself deep inside her. She wanted it. Just like that. No thought. Just action, instinct…lust.

"Adam," she groaned.

Julia. Her name tore into his heart, where he knew better.

She deserved more than a quick outdoor slam-bam-thank-you-ma'am. In his parents' back yard, of all places.

"Wait," he said. "Julia. Wait." He held her face between his hands. "Stop."

She screwed her eyes shut, as if not looking would mean not understanding. "Don't you dare." She was forcing each word from between gritted teeth. "Don't you dare—"

He stroked her cheeks.

"Don't say it." Her eyes flashed open. "I am not your mistake!"

He hesitated.

She made a sound of fury and pressed her lips hard against his. "Kiss me." Her mouth moved, softening, plucking at his. "This isn't wrong. See how good it feels?"

Good didn't equal right in his outlook, but he couldn't disagree with her. Not when she was stringing precious kisses across his face, each one as perfect as a pearl. It had been so long since he'd felt this kind of tenderness accompanying his desire, right alongside the honest need of a woman, burning bright and pure. Coming on the heels of their first hot embrace, such an emotional reaction felt even more dangerous. It was insidious as it worked its way under his skin, making him want her with his heart as much as his body. Pleasure and comfort, coaxing him into succumbing to his weakness for her.

He fought it. Wrenched his mouth away from the sweetness of hers.

She nestled her face against his shoulder. Her hand crept along his heaving chest, patting him, petting him. "Doesn't it feel good?"

He couldn't bring himself to push her away. "Of course it does." His sigh was ragged.

"But?" she whispered. Reluctantly.

"You know..."

"Zack." She twisted her head in denial, her hand making a fist upon his chest. "When are you going to realize that it doesn't matter to him? He has no claim on me."

"But he did. And we... We broke his trust."

With a tired groan, she straightened, brushed her hair. "Adam, that was so many years ago."

"You don't feel guilty?"

"I did. Of course I did."

"Past tense," he said, edging away so their legs didn't touch.

"Is it wrong to move on? Isn't that what you did?"

Literally, yes.

"After you left," she said, "I tried. I stayed with Zack, pretending to be the perfect girlfriend. But don't you see? It was just—" She started to reach for him, then folded her hands and tucked them beneath her chin instead. "It was hollow. Meaningless. After being with you, I knew what it was to feel truly alive. I wanted to be that way again, to *feel,* even if that meant I was also going to feel horribly guilty for a long while."

He steeled himself against her nearness, her words. "You didn't tell Zack everything."

"No." She took a breath. "Since you weren't around, I couldn't come entirely clean about...us. But I owed Zack at least part of the truth, so I confessed that I'd developed certain feelings for another man and didn't feel comfortable about the, uh, situation." Her smile was bleak and distant when she glanced at him. "Trust me, Adam. Zack wasn't terribly distraught about the breakup. We'd been running on fumes for months by then."

Adam studied the river, slate gray beneath the darkening sky. Damn if his hungry need for her wasn't still running rampant through his veins, strong enough to bust his zipper along with his will. Carefully he leaned forward and put his elbows on his knees, trying hard not to look at Julia.

She'd broken up with Zack. Not only because of their betrayal. Because she'd been halfway in love with Adam.

It was a revelation. Their sexual escapade had meant more to her than just a stupid, rash, regrettable teenage mistake.

"You're saying that you and Zack might not have lasted anyway?" He couldn't quite keep the rising hope out of his voice.

Julia's eyes went wide as she carefully thought that over. "I don't know for sure. We might have gone on, made ourselves a marriage of best friends."

His inhale felt like the stab of a knife.

"Though I can't imagine it would have lasted."

He exhaled in glorious relief.

"It might have been comfortable, but it wouldn't have been...satisfying." She slid over to lean lightly against him, searching for his gaze. "Is that what you need to hear? That my breakup with Zack wasn't all your fault?"

"I want you to tell the truth."

She touched his hand. "The truth..."

He waited, but she didn't continue. He wasn't sure, but there seemed to be an odd light in her eyes, as if ultimately she couldn't bring herself to trust him with it.

Why should she, he wondered bitterly. He'd run off before. He'd told her that he intended to do it again, just as soon as he could. Aside from their one memorable tryst, Julia was too cautious to commit herself to someone so unstable.

He turned his hand, pressed his palm against hers, matched her fingertips, silently thrilled that she didn't pull away.

"Adam, Madman, wild man," she murmured, refusing to reach for him, just holding her hand in place against his. "You're not so very dangerous, after all."

6

THE FIRST KISS was tentative. Barely a brushing of their lips.

Adam couldn't let himself believe it. Julia wanted him to kiss her. Him!

She smelled like wildflowers. Her loose hair brushed against his cheek when he leaned in for another kiss, his hands trembling as he lifted them to her shoulders. He wasn't sure he dared to touch her, but suddenly he was doing just that, his mouth on hers and his hands sliding along her arms as he gathered her to pull her closer, so close he felt her breasts shift against his chest as she swallowed, heard the sandpaper moan at the back of her throat. "Goldie," he said against her mouth. His heartbeat was a sledgehammer in his chest. "I always wanted—"

She interrupted, her eyes opening wide. "This is wrong." Her fingers tangled in his hair. She let out a sound of sheer frustration and then flung herself at him with an almost violent passion, crying out as their mouths clashed. "And I don't care!"

He couldn't make himself stop kissing her. "But what about Zack?"

"It's not happening between us," she said, her eyes as hot and wild and desperate as her hands. She stripped away his shirt. "We're too much alike."

"But this is wrong. You said—"

"I don't care." She wrapped her arms around his neck and let her head fall back, her hair swinging free. "I don't want to play it safe." He kissed her arched throat, felt her pulse pounding beneath his lips. She shimmied against him, hunching her shoulders as his mouth lowered to the warm valley between her breasts. "For once I want to be reckless, like you."

They fell onto the bed.

"WHAT GOES UP must come down," Adam said, patient with Julia's apprehension while she fiddled with the harness, checking the spring-loaded gates on the carabiners for the hundredth time.

She flexed her cold hands; they felt stiff and awkward, and she swore she couldn't feel her fingertips. "Going down is a lot scarier."

"Depends on the destination."

She squinted an eye at him. A smile teased his lips, daring her to flirt back.

Oh, Adam. She tucked her hands into her armpits. Why was she so taken with him? He was often prickly and remote. His hair was unkempt, his clothes were atrocious—a purple hooded jacket from high school and jeans that had bypassed comfortably worn and gone straight to thoroughly disreputable. He was layered in rock dust from head to toe. Yet he exuded enough sex appeal to make even her numb fingertips tingle. She'd been blowing off work to go rock climbing with him for five days in a row.

"It's not the destination, it's the speed," she said,

veering toward safety. "Falling's not my worry. Falling fast is."

He shot an evaluating look over his shoulder as he bent to straighten a kink in the webbing of the anchor. "I'm keeping hold of you, Goldie. I'll let you down slow and easy."

This time, she thought, her pulse picking up speed. She still remembered waking up in the motel room—alone. She'd hit the ground with a thud that had broken her heart.

"You ready?"

"Give me another minute."

"The longer you hesitate the tougher it'll be to force yourself over the edge." He slapped her on the back-side. The carabiners jingled. "Get moving."

The swat made her hop forward, close enough to the ledge to peer over. It was astonishing that she'd managed the ascension with relative ease. Naturally, the climb had been easy for Adam, like all the rest. Ever since Thornhill she'd been watching him closely, overlooking a lot of her hesitancy in the process. As a result, in the past several days her skills had improved to the point where she'd begun to enjoy the process and not only the accomplishment. She was beginning to understand how easy it was to get hooked on the adrenaline rush of escalating challenges.

Taller, steeper, higher.

Touch me, hug me, kiss me....

She shook her head. Rappelling was another matter. She'd made a couple of super-short rappels and had shaken like a leaf the entire trip south. Going up, even with the backup of the belay line, she relied on herself, be that for good or bad. Going down, she had to lean on the ropes and depend that the anchor at the top would hold her secure. Scary stuff for a control queen.

Adam jogged the line. "C'mon, Goldie. We haven't got all day. It's cold up here. Let's get out of the wind."

"Let me just..." she mumbled, slipping on a pair of gloves. At least things had changed between her and Adam. It was as if their kisses had broken the ice that kept them frozen around each other, and now they could breathe and move again without being painfully aware of every little nuance. In a way, they were friends again.

In another way, they were not.

She tugged at the harness biting into her hips and groin, thinking of how her breath had caught short when Adam buckled her into it, even though his hands had been professionally detached as he touched her in intimate spots and turned her this way and that to check and double-check. Maybe they weren't as awkward with each other, but they were still striking sparks. It was hell, biding her time while he got used to the idea that she wasn't nearly as off-limits as he'd made her out to be.

"Okay," she said. Deep breath. "Here I go." She gripped the rope, sought his eyes and gave a shaky laugh. "Don't let go."

He held her gaze. "Don't you look down."

She leaned against the harness, letting it bear her weight. "I have to. I have to see where I'm going."

"No, you don't. Keep looking at me. Let your feet do the work, not your eyes."

She concentrated on his face so intently it seemed as if

there was a stream of energy flowing between them. Gradually his confidence filled her, building her up until she was able to back herself over the side. The rubber soles of her shoes scraped against the vertical stone as she tested each step. The harness tightened around her legs. She let out the rope a tiny bit, giving herself leeway.

The wind whistled. Suddenly she was aware of the empty space swirling below her. Of the long drop to the ground and the seeming insignificance of the devices holding her up.

Adam's voice reached out to her. "Look at me, Julia."

She nodded. He was steadfast, standing well back from the ledge she teetered on.

"You can do it. Easy as a piece of warm pumpkin pie."

"If I had pie in me, I'd be puking it up." She gave herself another inch of rope.

He chuckled. "Flex your knees, honey. You're too stiff. And lean farther back. You want to be almost horizontal."

Her knee joints felt as creaky as an antique rocking chair. She bounced a little, the way Adam had demonstrated. Her stomach dropped when the rope moved with her and she lifted slightly off the rock face. "Yipes," she squeaked as she rebounded, her feet scrambling for solid purchase.

"There you go," Adam said. "Felt good, didn't it?"

She craned her neck at him. "Are you crazy?"

"Try it again. Give yourself more rope."

"It's too...too..."

"Exhilarating? Liberating?"

She snorted.

"C'mon, Jule," he coaxed. "Remember when you were a girl, flipping around the monkey bars with your braids flying? Let yourself soar like that again."

She darted a glance at the distant ground. "But I like being earthbound. Gravity is my friend."

"Nope. Gravity is one surly bad-ass dude. But you're going to get your cute little behind in gear and thumb your nose at him while you swing down this rock like a ballet dancer."

"What happened to the pie?"

He chuckled. "Quit stalling."

Okay, a ballet dancer. Right. She leaned against the harness, swaying a little. Her feet shifted. A small chunk of rock broke off beneath her heel and bounced down the cliffside exactly the way she imagined herself doing whenever she lost eye contact with Adam. A few more steps and she'd have dipped below his sight line. She wouldn't be able to see him at all.

"Are you the same bridesmaid who wanted to defy death?"

"Maid of honor," she said, biting down on her chattering teeth. She had to do it. He was the kind of teacher who'd leave her dangling like a spider on a string, tossed back and forth between the wind and the rocks.

"Maid of honor," he repeated.

"Yeah, and I'm one surly bad-ass maid of honor," she muttered. "Don't mess with me."

"That's the spirit."

She raised the volume. "Okay! I'm going!"

Adam waited. She didn't move.

"I dare you," he said.

"Dare me? Nope. A dare's not doing it for me," she said through cold lips. "I need more than that." Every muscle strained to hold her position. She was going to have to move soon, one way or the other.

"Promise yourself a reward, then, but get your behind moving. If I have to lower you inch by inch, I'm never taking you climbing again."

"There's only one reward I want," she said, "and you won't give it to me." She inched lower as she spoke, but she did it on legs that were stiff and awkward. He was right; she wanted grace, freedom, bounding joy. She wanted to soar.

He stretched his neck for another glimpse of her. "Whatever you want. I promise."

She tipped her head, sighting herself on his face for one exhilarating instant before she let the rope slide through her hands. Her knees flexed, and she sailed up and out, arcing over the rock. The freedom of movement was intoxicating. She bounced off the balls of her feet and did it again, even bigger, the rope vibrating in her hand. "My God," she whispered, finding her rhythm. The rope sang to her as she glided down it, bounding against the rock face, all the way to the ground, the adrenaline igniting her enthusiasm like fiery bursts of a Fourth of July sparkler.

She landed harder than she'd intended, stumbling against the sudden reality of solid ground. The earth tilted. "Whew." Her balance wobbled back and forth, righting itself after the glorious freedom. When she was steady, she unhooked herself, took a step back and shouted to Adam that she was off the line.

Far above, he stood at the edge of the cliff, looking at

her. He was silhouetted against the pale sun and flat gray sky; the sight of him made her heart lift, rising on wings to reach him.

She waved. He held up a clenched fist, shouting something she couldn't quite hear, because of the distance or the singing in her bloodstream, she didn't care. She was a rock climber! Adam was with her. Could life get any better than that?

He zipped down to join her, agile as a mountain goat. Even before he got his bearings and unhooked, she went to him. She flung herself into his arms with none of her normal reserve and hugged him with a tight enthusiasm, giddy enough to giggle.

"Thanks for browbeating me. That was amazing!"

"*You* are amazing." His restless hands moved over her back.

"I was free as a bird."

"A bird in straps and buckles. Maybe you ought to try skydiving, after all."

She dropped down off her toes, becoming more aware of their positioning. *Yum.* "I ought to."

The air was charged with their electricity; it felt prickly against her skin. She cupped Adam's face. Beneath a frowning brow, his eyes darkened, but she didn't think he was warning her off. She didn't think. Didn't want to....

Her lips parted, settling upon his with a tiny wet sound. He tasted like the wind, the rock. The tip of her tongue touched his teeth, and they unclenched, allowing her to deepen the kiss. She flicked her tongue against his in a heady swirl of sensation.

She felt as though pure oxygen had been pumped

into her hollowed-out bones. She was as light as air. She ended the kiss in a sweet horizontal slide of her lips over Adam's, trailing several small kisses along the edge of his jaw. Then she threw back her head and opened her arms and laughed at the sky.

Adam seemed ambiguous, waiting for her to calm down. He grabbed a fistful of her jacket and held her steady while he stroked her hair, petting the loose strands behind her ears. "I've created a monster."

She shook her head, letting the strands that had come loose from her ponytail fly every which way. "*You've* created? I don't think so. I'm my own creation. This was all my idea."

"Good. Then I can't be blamed."

She sobered. "I'm not looking to place blame."

"Not even next week, or next month, when—"

Her palm pressed against his mouth. "Hush."

He nodded.

She kissed him again, quickly.

"That was your reward," he said, unthreading the rope at his waist.

"I never said that."

His head came up sharply. "No?"

"You think I'm so beholden to your masculine charisma that a kiss from you is all the reward I would ask for?" She scoffed. "The women of this town have fed you Brody men far too much admiration."

Adam unbuckled the harness and let it drop to the ground like a gunslinger's holster. He swept her into his arms and kissed her quite soundly and very thoroughly, until he'd stolen all the oxygen from her lungs and even her bones. She let herself lean against him, enjoying the moment for what it was. A whole bunch of kisses. Sexy, feel-good kisses. The kind that were meant to lead nowhere but right where they were—in each other's arms, enjoying their mutual attraction without bowing to the oppression of being furtive, guilty lovers.

"Then this is *my* reward," Adam murmured against her lips.

"Yes, all yours."

She felt him tighten, then purposely relax. "Right," he said with a sigh, gently setting her away. "We'd better be on our way. The sun's going down."

"What about my reward?" she said, helping him organize the climbing gear.

"Be reasonable," he cautioned.

"It's not too terrible. All I want is an invitation to the Brody Thanksgiving." On the surface, it wasn't much of a request. Mrs. Brody's invitations tended to be open-ended, anyhow. But this time Julia needed to know that Adam would be okay with her attending. There'd already been talk around town about how often they were seen together. Any perceptive observer, even at a big, raucous event like a Brody holiday dinner, would see what was happening between her and Adam as soon as they got near each other. A Thanksgiving dinner invitation could wind up being the next best thing to a public declaration.

"You're crazy," Adam said. "All the relations are coming, and every stray soul my mother meets in the street. Dad's threatening to deep-fry one of the turkeys." He slid a wary glance over her. "Zack and Cathy are back. They'll be there."

"I know. Haven't I told you that I approve one hundred percent of their marriage?"

"That's not what I meant."

"Um. I see." She peeled off the gloves and rubbed her hands together. He knew what the invitation would signify as well as she did.

Adam looped the ropes around his shoulder. His ruddy face had grown a shade paler. "I'll have to talk to Zack about this."

Finally, she thought, faintly nervous at the prospect. She shrugged and said, "Yeah," for Adam's benefit. He wouldn't want to make it into a big deal, even though it was a conversation they should have had ten years ago.

A SWEATY MALE BODY hurled through the air and slammed into Adam like a sack of wet cement. His feet flew out from beneath him, and he landed on his backside on the polished wood floor, skidding a good three feet to the baseline. The basketball spun around the rim before dropping through the net. Someone yelled, "Foul!" Others cheered.

Pain radiated from Adam's tailbone. He laid his head on the gym floor with a groan. "Hell, Fred. This isn't tackle football."

Zack pulled up, panting, and squatted beside his brother. "Can you move?" Serious concern threaded his voice.

Adam waved him off. "Of course I can move. I just don't want to. I was head-butted by the biggest butt on the court."

Fred Spangler lumbered over, his sneakers squeaking on the slick floor. "Oh, man, oh, man, I'm sorry. I forgot.

Here, give me your hand, li'l bro." He held his out, then thought better and wiped it on his sweatshirt before offering it a second time.

Adam took it, letting Fred hoist him onto his feet even though the pain sliced through him like hot steel. "Don't apologize. I'm fine." He tightened his grip, crushing Fred's fingers. "But that was a foul, Shirley T."

Fred's eyes bulged beneath the corkscrew yellow curls that had earned him the nickname. "Yeah, yeah, yeah. A foul."

Adam released Fred's hand and clapped him on the back. "Next time, tackle someone your own size."

Out of breath, Fred doubled over to lean his arms on his thighs while he panted. "Chuck quit the league. Knee operation."

"We're all getting older," Zack said, tossing the basketball down the court to the rest of their group. He looked as healthy and fit as Captain America.

"Aren't you s'posed to come back tired from a honeymoon?" Fred complained between gasps. "Oh, man. I gotta get in better shape." He pressed a palm to his bulging midsection and staggered to the bench.

"Why don't you sit out for a while?" Zack said to his younger brother. "Keep Fred company."

Adam moved in a stiff circle, testing his hip. "It was just a spill. Took it on my tailbone."

"You've been overexerting."

"Been working myself back into shape.

"The doctors didn't tell you to do it all at once."

"A year and a half is more than enough time."

"Only a couple, maybe three weeks since you started climbing again."

"Thanks for keeping track, Mommy."

Zack scowled.

Adam pulled the bandanna off his head and used it to wipe the clammy sweat from his face and neck and hands. "I've been doing easy climbs at Julia's speed. Not what I'd call overexertion."

"Maybe it is. You're starting at the beginning again, whether or not you want to admit it." Zack turned away, muttering beneath his breath, "Thank God for Julia." He walked to the row of bleachers, forcing Adam to follow.

"What did you say about Julia?" he demanded. Fred looked up, interested. Zack shrugged.

The slam of the bouncing ball echoed in the largely empty gym, site of Zack's high-school heroics. The other three men had grown impatient. "Hey, Heartbreak. Are we gonna play or are we gonna sit around on our cans?"

Zack motioned to Fred. "Go two-on-two for a while." The beefy car salesman groaned but obediently heaved himself off the bench and jogged over to rejoin the game.

"Did you set the whole thing up?" Adam asked, sitting gingerly on the first bleacher. Zack was one row higher, his feet propped on the bottom bleacher as he watched the other men pound up and down the court. When he didn't answer, Adam shook his head. "I should have known. Julia's not the type to suddenly develop a craving for rock climbing and skydiving."

"What do you mean? She's always been athletic."

"Tennis. Cheerleading. Golf. Swimming. Clean, pretty, safe." Adam ticked the sports off, recalling quite clearly the sight of her in short skirts with fuzzy little pom-poms on her socks. She'd worn a yellow bikini to the Mirror Lake public beach throughout her sixteenth summer, the year she'd hooked up with Zack. Every boy in town had been infatuated, including Adam, although he'd tried not to consciously acknowledge just how frequently she'd made appearances in his racy adolescent fantasies.

But Julia at sixteen was unforgettable. A dream girl. Sweet-natured, friendly, with light blond hair and long legs, lightly tanned, smooth as silk. He'd touched them for the first time one hot summer night when she and Zack and a few of their friends had come to the quarry pond to swim. Adam had been camping there, relishing the solitude, but he couldn't complain when Julia apologized for the interruption and asked him to join them for a swim. The boys had started flipping the girls off their shoulders. Laurel Barnard, playing Veronica to Julia's Betty all that summer, had clung on to Zack, so Julia dragged Adam over to join in. Riveted by the contact as she climbed onto his shoulders, he'd turned his head, touching his cheek to her inner thigh for the briefest of moments before flipping her off backward with a huge splash. Maybe she'd known. He'd always wondered about that. And remembered the fleeting touch.

"You two thought I needed a baby-sitter," Adam speculated. He was resentful but not bitter. They'd had his safety in mind. And let's face it, they'd been right. He'd needed the extra time to reclaim his skills while gradually building his strength. His solo attempt at Thornhill had proved that.

Zack raked his hair. "You're wrong, Adam. Julia and

I didn't conspire. I'll grant you that we might have if I'd thought of it, but..."

"Come clean, brother. You've always been my keeper, rescuing me from scrapes, covering for me with Mom and Dad. You even ditched your own wedding to help me out after the accident." Adam's stomach cramped, thinking of the debt he owed to Zack. There was no way he could ever repay his brother for all that he'd done. Learning to accept help had been as hard a lesson for him as admitting his helplessness.

But *had* he learned it?

Zack brushed off the attempt at gratitude, as he usually did when Adam offered it. "You know that was just a convenient excuse for me to escape Laurel's clutches."

Adam nodded grimly, thinking back. The worst part of the ordeal wasn't that he'd been foolish enough to become infatuated with a schemer like Laurel, it was that she hadn't told him she was pregnant with his baby. She'd then wangled a marriage proposal out of Zack, playing on his sense of honor to give the baby a proper last name. Mere weeks before the wedding, the plan had begun to go awry when she'd suffered a miscarriage. Adam had learned all of this after the fact—reason enough, or so he'd thought, to stay away from conniving females for good.

"Nope," Zack said with his usual firm, open conviction. "The rock-climbing lessons were all Julia's doing."

Adam had to believe him; his brother didn't lie. "Why would she risk herself?" he wondered out loud, extending her the benefit of the doubt because he couldn't imagine Julia conniving. She was too good for that.

Zack gave him a look. "You might want to ask her."

Dangerous territory. Adam shifted on the hard surface of the bleachers, wincing at the twinges that came from his sore backside. "Uh, I'll do that."

They watched the game in silence for a few moments, until one of Fred's flailing elbows smacked another player in the eye, and the action ceased among more cries of "Foul!"

"How's Julia managing?" Zack ventured. "I can't quite picture it."

"She's pretty good," Adam admitted. "Improving every climb, especially since I got her to loosen up and trust in herself." He remembered the joy on her face when she'd rappelled down the craggy rocks with springs in her heels, forgetting her fear and bounding as lightly as a deer through a fallow pasture. They'd been out once since then, and she'd been positively daring, channeling all her pent-up physical—perhaps sexual—energy into the climb. "Wouldn't surprise me if she did decide to try skydiving, after all," he said. Especially if shots of adrenaline were an antidote to their idling relationship.

Zack's brows rose. "Really? That's not the Julia I know. She's always been so..." He spread his hands.

"So grounded," Adam supplied. *Safe, settled, careful.*

"Like me." Zack grinned. "We always were too much alike."

Adam shrugged. He didn't want to think about Zack and Julia together, even though this was the perfect opportunity to lay all his cards on the table.

Zack's head tilted. "Wonder what's gotten into her, then."

Not me, Adam thought, feeling as tense as if a scalding needle had been thrust into his spine. *At least not yet.* He groaned silently at himself. *I'm a worm. Forgive me, Zack.*

"She blames it on your wedding," he said, sounding strangled.

Zack blinked. "Not because—"

"No, no. Don't worry. She's over you."

"I knew that." Zack was sheepish. "Cathy's been more than willing to remind me that I'm not nearly the heartbreaker I'd been made out to be. I think she's disappointed."

With a short laugh, Adam cuffed him on the shoulder. "Doubt that." Anyone who'd seen them together since they'd gotten back from their honeymoon would have.

Zack had the grace to look even more sheepish. "So explain to me about Julia," he said to change the subject.

Adam stared at his hands, dangling between his knees. With his new wife, Zack's protective nature was roused to an even greater degree. He treated Cathy like a precious jewel, catering to her every want and need. Adam teased him about it, but the truth was that being around the pair made him feel more alone than the time he'd bivouacked in the Himalayas without a soul in sight for endless miles.

"What's the wedding got to do with her rock climbing?" Zack prodded.

"I don't know." Adam laced his fingers, trying to focus on Julia's needs instead of his wants. "Something about restlessness and change, I guess. She said she's bored with her life. Wants to shake it up."

"Julia, bored? Hmm." Zack rubbed the tip of his nose, his forehead wrinkling. "I suppose it's possible. But she looked really happy when I ran into her in Cathy's shop yesterday. Cathy mentioned it, too. There's a certain zip in her step and a sparkle in her—"

He stopped and looked at Adam. And smiled.

"What?" Adam said, sitting straight. Heat crawled up his throat.

"What, what? You two have been seeing a lot of each other, that's all."

"It's not—" Adam swallowed. It *was* like that.

He peered over his shoulder at his brother. "You can quit smiling now."

Zack sobered like a judge, except for the reddened tip of his nose and his dancing eyes. He nudged Adam with his toe.

"Pest." Out of an old impulse to needle his older brother, Adam pulled a curly brown hair out of Zack's calf.

"Ow." Zack snaked an arm around Adam's neck from behind, gripping him in a headlock. Adam twisted; Zack's hold tightened. They tussled on the bleachers for a minute, the struggle punctuated with mild oaths, insults and grunts.

"Ooh, my back," Adam said at one point, which gave Zack a split-second pause, enabling the younger brother to escape his grasp. "Psych," he said, repeating their old teenage taunt.

"Brat." Zack chased him onto the court.

Light on his feet, Adam easily evaded him. "Slowing

down, old man?" he taunted, bouncing from side to side. "Or is Cathy wearing you out?"

Zack made a grab and missed. "Damn. You're moving better than ever." He stopped and sopped off his face with the edge of his old basketball jersey. "Bet you don't need the cane at all anymore."

Adam rested his hands on his hips. "Not in a week, maybe ten days." Liar. He remembered exactly when he last used it—the day he'd left Julia's in such pain. "But I keep it around, in case."

"Still doing the stretching exercises?"

"Yes, Nurse Brody."

"Just checking."

"I get sore. Whirlpool baths take the kinks out."

Zack nodded. "Mom's thrilled that you're staying home longer this time. Don't be surprised if she persuades Julia to lure you into more lessons."

Adam glanced at the players. "I'm leaving after Thanksgiving." Definitely. Right after Thanksgiving.

Zack's expression clouded, but he didn't protest. "Then we'd better make it a good Thanksgiving."

"Uh..." Adam scuffed his sneaker against the gym floor. "Uh, somehow Julia's been invited. Is that okay with you?"

"Sure, it is." Zack seemed taken aback, but Adam couldn't tell if it was because she'd been invited or because there was no question she was welcome.

Zack's brows arched at the silence that grew between them, uncomfortable on Adam's side, curious on his brother's. "As your date?" he finally asked, caught halfway between teasing and seriousness.

"Not exactly." Adam winced. "Well, yeah, sort of."

"Good," Zack said. He laid his hand on Adam's shoulder and gave it a squeeze. "Good for both of you."

Adam exhaled. It wasn't everything; the air wasn't completely cleared. Julia was expecting him to dig deep into the subject, to come totally clean. And he would. But for now, he looped an arm around Zack's shoulders and walked along the basketball court with him, feeling lighter inside than he had in ages.

It wasn't everything, but for the moment it was enough.

SCARBOROUGH FAIRE, Cathy Brody's arts and crafts shop on Central Street, was the hangout of the group of women who'd once called themselves the Heartbroken because each one, to varying degrees, had loved and lost Zack "Heartbreak" Brody. At one time, Julia, Gwendolyn Case, Faith Fagan, Allie Spangler and Laurel Barnard had formed the core group. It had been Laurel's idea to set Cathy up with Zack, but the plan for revenge had backfired when love struck the pair instead of revenge. Now the group had dwindled. Laurel and Faith were infrequent visitors. Allie, who had abandoned her previous jealousy over her childhood crush and was concentrating on making her marriage to Fred work, still showed up, although the calligraphy course had ended. The current craze was scrapbooking.

Julia wasn't particularly into scrapbooking, but she came for the camaraderie. Everyone else in the group had photos of family fun and frolics to fill their pages. Most of the photos in Julia's life were the ones she took of her real-estate listings. Allie, meaning to be helpful, had suggested that she make pages out of her high-school memories, but that had been just too much living in the past for her to contemplate. Instead, she was working on a wedding page for Cathy. The orange tulle bridesmaid dresses deserved to be commemorated in infamy.

The main topic of the evening was Laurel Barnard. Her Quimby social status had suffered after her truly nasty nature was revealed. However, now that the wedding was past, it was safe for her to return from exile—which in Laurel's case was a long Mediterranean cruise. Karen Thompson, who'd been running the dress shop, reported that Laurel had shown up with a new haircut, a sunburn and a mysterious suitor named Franco who'd already sent flowers, chocolates and, rather weirdly, a complete set of sterling-silver bathroom accessories. It figured, they'd all agreed. Since Laurel was a catty bitch, she *would* land on her feet.

"Nine o'clock," Cathy announced eventually. "Time to pack up our scissors and croppers for another day."

"Just one more," said Philly Weston, a plump young woman who was using the scalloped scissors. Julia remembered that Philly was single, too—in fact, she'd stood up for all to see and rather boldly bid on Zack during Quimby's famous Founder's Day bachelor auction.

The other women were getting ready to leave. "Ooh, almost finished," Philly said, cutting madly. Julia leaned closer to look. The exuberant young woman was scalloping a photo of herself and two girlfriends posing in turquoise waters with tanks, masks and fins.

"Scuba diving," Julia said. "Hey, I should try that."

Allie made a face. "And give up rock climbing?"

"You can't break a leg in the water," Gwen observed, packing her scrapbook gear into a hefty carryall that she slung over her shoulder. Normally, she lingered until the last, to be certain she'd inhaled every crumb of gossip, but tonight she had a late date with Cathy's dad, the admiral. He claimed it took more than a bridal bouquet to scare away a Navy man.

Although the group had been giving Julia a ribbing over her unexpected foray into adventure sports, so far they hadn't figured out that the lessons meant more to her than climbing and rappelling. Naturally, their curiosity about Adam was rampant. They'd dissected his personality and come to the general consensus that, despite the appeal of the untamable, his worth as a long-term prospect was nil.

Eventually the women gathered the last of their scrapbook materials and departed. Even Philly, who trailed scraps of scalloped paper all the way out the door. Julia lingered, helping Cathy clean off the worktable and set the candy-striped, polka-dotted chairs on it upside down so the floor could be swept. As long as she had the push broom, a wide, industrial model, she made a quick sweep of the rest of the colorful, chaotic shop. The harvest display in the front window was shedding straw dust and slender threads of corn silk.

"Nearly done," she said, taking the broom down the center aisle to pick up Philly's leavings. Cathy turned off most of the lights and locked the front door. Julia went to the storeroom and tipped the dustpan into the garbage. She rinsed her hands and came out drying them on a paper towel to find Cathy eyeing a big gooey fudge brownie, the last one left in the grease-spotted bakery box.

"Split it with you." Julia had already eaten one brownie, but it wasn't enough. Ever since the wedding, she'd been craving chocolate like mad. Aunt Delilah must have been right about its giddy-up properties.

"We gorged on the honeymoon. Now I'm on a diet." Cathy touched her flat midriff. "I have this fear that being happily married will make me gain weight. After years of deprivation and Lean Cuisine, I keep wanting to cook these lovely, scrumptious, fattening meals for Zack. All the women in my family did it, except for some reason the husbands stayed skinny while the wives got plump."

"My theory is that testosterone burns calories. Estrogen clings to them like life rafts. It's God's little practical joke on womankind."

"I had more nervous energy when I was single." Cathy tasted a dollop of chocolate frosting and rolled her eyes. "Now I'm settled, and so has my metabolism."

Julia laughed. "Oh, I feel for you. Gimme that brownie. I'll eat it, even though you have a better way of working it off than I do."

Cathy closed her eyes and thrust her face aside as if she couldn't bear to look while she handed the treat over to Julia. "Take it—take it far away!"

Julia sat on a corner of the table, holding the box beneath her chin while she wolfed down the brownie. Her nervous energy was burning hotter than ever.

Cathy watched ruefully. "You'll probably have to climb the Thornhill cliffs to burn away that many calories."

"I want to try it. But Adam's being a stick."

"That's rare."

Julia licked her fingers. "What do you mean?"

"Adam, playing it safe. Isn't his nickname Madman?" Cathy started putting the chairs down. "I suppose his injuries are holding him back."

"Not so you'd notice," Julia murmured, scrunching her chin. She sucked a tiny sliver of macadamia nut from between her teeth.

"Then he's watching out for you. He *cares* for you."

Julia intercepted Cathy's speculative glance. "You're fishing."

"Sure am." Cathy plopped into a chair painted with pink swirls and yellow stars. She was equally colorful, dressed in a loose, tie-dyed jumper. "I'm dying to know if anything's happening between you two. It's dreadful not being able to say anything when the others are around."

"I appreciate your discretion. If Gwen got an inkling, any chance I have with Adam would be sunk for good. He doesn't take well to being talked about."

Cathy folded her hands beneath her chin, leaning forward on her elbows. "So you do have a chance?"

Julia nodded demurely. She felt all shivery inside.

"I knew it!"

Julia turned and dropped onto one of the chairs. "You can't tell Zack." She gripped the edge of the table. "I know I shouldn't ask you to keep a secret from your husband, but it's better if we let Adam tell him."

"Yeeowch." Cathy winced. "I don't know...."

"It's complicated. More than I've let you in on."

Cathy wasn't pushy. She waited, her head cocked expectantly.

Julia settled back, pulled two ways. Cathy had grown to become her best friend in the year or so since she'd moved to Quimby. But Julia's loyalty—no, loyalty wasn't the word. Her allegiance was with Adam. They'd shared their secret for so long, it was an unspoken pact of silence between them.

Still, she trusted Cathy implicitly. And she really needed to talk it out, to confess her sin so she could shed it and to figure out if it would even matter to Zack.

Cathy would know, if anyone did.

Julia straightened her cuffs. She smoothed her hair. She said in a flat monotone, "I cheated on Zack. With Adam."

Cathy was nearly successful at muffling her gasp.

Julia squeezed her eyes shut. "Ten years ago, July nineteenth, my eighteenth birthday."

Silence. Then, "Oh, Julia..."

There was sympathy in Cathy's voice, not censure. Julia's lids flew up. "You don't automatically hate me?"

"There's more to the story, I expect."

"Those are the essential facts. The rest is prevarication. Excuses." Julia looked at her hands, folded tightly in her lap. "And I know Adam—he's boiled it down to the same thing. We cheated on his brother. There can be no forgiveness."

"Of course there can, given the reasons. Especially now, after so much time has passed."

"Zack is such a good guy. So decent."

Cathy nodded. "Yes. And that means he'll give you a chance to explain."

"The time to explain was when it happened. Instead, Adam and I pretended it didn't happen at all." Julia gave a mirthless laugh. "As if we could go back to the way we were before."

"I don't understand. Was this the reason you and Zack broke up?"

"Yes. More or less. I finally found the guts to tell him that I'd fallen for someone else. By then, it was clear to both of us that we weren't quite the perfect couple as billed by all of Quimby."

Cathy was concerned. "Tell me how it happened."

Before launching into the story, Julia glanced around the dim shop. The street was totally quiet; downtown Quimby rolled the sidewalks up at night. No better time for a confession.

"Zack and I had been dating for two years. I thought I was in love with him, but I was a teenager—" she smiled wryly "—and more impulsive and emotional than I am now. Looking back, I think I was half in love with his home and family, though of course Zack was a big part of that.

"So, anyway, I'd just graduated and was planning to go to the same college as Zack. My eighteenth birthday arrived that summer, and there I was—still a virgin."

Cathy looked startled. "We're talking about the same Zack Brody?"

"He respected me."

"Oh, you poor thing."

Julia nodded, her head drooping. "I thought he was being honorable about it, and we *were* separated all that school year when he left for college. In retrospect, our impressive restraint should have been another clue that we weren't meant for each other." She tucked her bobbed hair behind her ears. "Don't get me wrong—we'd experimented. Zack was a damn good kisser—"

Cathy grinned. "Still is."

"You're not jealous?"

"Not really. But then I've had time to get accustomed to you all talking of Zack's legendary smooth moves." Cathy tapped her platinum wedding band. "Besides, I've got him now. For good." She laughed. "The Heartbroken can have their girlish memories."

"I *was* just a girl. But not completely naive. I'd been noticing Adam by then. Something about him..." Julia's gaze drifted.

Adam at eighteen. He'd been so different from his brother. Not suave, not polite, but raw and electric—an exposed nerve. He'd found a sense of inner calm since then, but at the time he'd been a jumble of reckless impulses and hormones. He'd touched a matching nerve in her, thrilling her, exposing her secret craving for danger instead of safety.

Julia came to the present with a shake. Cathy was watching her, nodding.

"To be honest, it was my attraction to Adam that got me...riled. Suddenly I didn't want to be a virgin anymore, so I very rationally came up with a plan to give Zack the big prize on the night of my eighteenth birthday. There was going to be a party with friends, and I booked a motel room for afterward. Stocked it with champagne and candles. It was going to be the epitome of romance."

Cathy smiled fondly. "Yeah, Julia, I can see you doing that. Everything just so."

"You know what they say about best-laid plans...." Julia groaned. "Toward the end of the party, I slipped out to prepare myself for the big event. I left a room key for Zack. Our rendezvous was going to be a surprise."

"Uh-oh," Cathy breathed, caught up in the story.

Julia nodded. "The wrong brother showed up. I'd left the key with Allie to give to Zack. But she'd been doing Jell-O shots and apparently was too busy throwing up in the ladies' room to pass it on directly. She gave it to Fred. From there the trail gets hazy."

"Was Laurel there?" Cathy's eyes narrowed to slits. "Wouldn't surprise me, given her history, if she'd redirected the key out of spite."

"I could never come right out and ask. Because of what wound up happening between me and Adam, it was too delicate a situation for me to go blundering about, demanding explanations. But from what I was able to find out, it was a simple misunderstanding. Fred wasn't paying attention and handed the key to the wrong brother."

"I see, I see. So Adam arrives at the room instead of Zack. He must have known you hadn't planned to seduce *him*, though. Right?"

"Yup."

"But...?"

"Well, we'd both done our fair share of drinking. And Adam and I did have this chemistry. It was hard to contain. I started crying on his shoulder about how Zack and I weren't the perfect couple everyone thought we were, and..." Julia put her hands over her face. "You know how it goes. Two eighteen-year-olds alone in a motel room. We kissed. And once we started we just—

we just..." She dropped her hands to the table with a thud. "We couldn't stop."

"Oh, my stars. And you were a virgin..."

"So was Adam. It was a powerful experience. Happy birthday to me."

"And afterward?"

"What else?" Julia threw up her hands. "Regret. Shame. Guilt."

"Oh," Cathy said, her pretty face riddled with concern as she turned the situation over in her mind. "Oh." She winced. "Oh, poor Zack..."

"Adam was devastated by what we'd done, even more than me. He idolizes Zack, so betraying him was—" Julia shrugged. "Even now, he can't imagine Zack forgiving him, which means he can't forgive himself. He's been torturing himself with that. All this time."

Cathy reached across the table for Julia's trembling hands. "There's no doubt that Zack would have been hurt. But if, as you say, you two truly weren't devoted..." She squeezed. "Zack's capacity for forgiveness amazes me. He doesn't even hold a grudge against Laurel! Me, I still want to scratch her eyes out." Cathy shook her head. "So I'm sure he'd understand how you and Adam might have—y'know. You were young. You acted rashly. It was just a mistake."

Julia recoiled. *Was it more than a mistake if after ten years she still replayed making love with Adam over and over again in her mind?*

Her thoughts were interrupted by a sharp rap at the

glass door. Both women rose from the table, craning to see who knocked.

Zack. Zack—handsome, blameless, smiling and waving hello.

All the blood drained from Julia's face.

7

FORGIVE ME. Adam mouthed the words. It was the last coherent thought in his brain. Julia's spontaneous passion had ignited him. He hadn't really known how powerful and deep his feelings for her ran, because he hadn't let himself know. But now...

His wildest fantasy had come true.

She wanted him.

And he was too far gone to say no.

His hands swept across her body. She writhed, arching into the caress, moving one of her long, bare legs between his. He slid his palm along her thigh. Such skin, she had. Such amazing skin. And he was touching it. Kissing it.

Damn, this was crazy!

She pressed hot kisses onto his chest. He rose on his elbows, searching for her mouth, the need to possess her drumming in his veins. They kissed again, and all his clumsy, frantic worry melted away as they began to move together, stripping away the rest of their clothing, every wiggle and shiver and shrug a full spectrum of sensation.

CATHY FLUTTERED fingers at her husband, who waited patiently at the door. "Zack's here. What are we going to do?"

"Nothing," Julia said. "Do nothing. Say nothing. Adam's going to talk to Zack. I've been invited for

Thanksgiving, and we thought it might feel weird, so they have to talk about the change in our relationships. It's overdue."

"But how can I—"

"You don't have to lie. Keep it to yourself. Like a priest hearing my confession."

Cathy was dubious. "I'll try," she said out of the side of her mouth, waving again.

Julia tucked her handbag under her arm and marched toward the exit. "I'm getting out of here as fast as I can. In the meantime, smile. You look like a plucked chicken."

Cathy followed. "He's going to know as soon as he looks at me."

"Stop making that face, then. You have nothing to feel guilty about." Julia twisted the lock and threw open the door. "Hiya, Zachary. I'm on my way. See ya!"

"Whoa, slow down," he said, gripping her by the shoulders. "What's the rush?"

Her mind raced. "I have a video to return. I'll have to pay late charges if I don't go right this very minute."

"Anything good?"

"*Cliffhanger,*" she blurted. "You know I have a, uh, thing for—" *mountain climbers?* "—Sylvester Stallone."

"Sure you do." Zack released her and turned to give Cathy a big hug that turned into a kiss. "Sorry I'm late, Cath. Our game ran long, but Adam finally broke it up to go in search of a whirlpool bath. Fred knocked him on his butt—"

Julia whirled in the middle of the street. "Is he hurt?

Behind Zack's back, Cathy motioned at her to take it down a notch.

"I mean, he's okay, isn't he? Fred's quite the load." Julia laughed awkwardly. "I wouldn't want to be run over by him, that's for darn tootin'."

Zack raised his brows at the corny expression that had fallen out of her mouth. It was one her father might use, not her. Despite her years as a cheerleader, she was no good at fake cheer. "Um, Adam seemed okay to me," he said. "Maybe you want to check on him."

"Right," Julia said. "I mean, wrong. No need for that, I'm sure. Oh, well, I was going, wasn't I?" She turned on her heel and scuttled off to her car, parked on the other side of the street near the drugstore.

"Have you girls been smoking the sphagnum moss again?" she heard Zack say before she slammed her car door. "That was not our usual calm, cool Julia."

THE EVERGREEN POINT show house was completely quiet.

Julia crept up the carpeted steps. If Zack hadn't given her a clue, she wouldn't have suspected Adam was there. His Jeep was nowhere in sight. Not a single light had shone through the windows.

She paused in the hallway, listening. It seemed as though she should hear the distant sounds of pulsing jets and swirling water, but there was nothing. Maybe Zack was wrong.

She stopped inside the doorway of the master bedroom and waited. Outside, the stars were clear and bright. The air had smelled wintry for the first time this year. A November chill clung to her jacket. She rubbed her hands together. *Why am I doing this?*

Because she wanted to be with Adam. All the time.

He consumed every waking thought and plenty of the sleeping ones, too.

The bathroom door had been left partly open. She moved through the dark bedroom, every sense keen with anticipation. Ten years ago, she'd been overwhelmed with teenage emotions and lust. This time, she was a mature woman making a deliberate decision. Still, the outcome was the same.

She wanted to be with Adam.

Julia touched the door. No sounds came from the bathroom, but her nerve endings were tellingly jumpy, a sure sign that he was close. Breathing deep, she caught a slight whiff of his unique scent. Only a trace, but it was enough to make her nostrils flare and her throat contract. Her body thrummed with arousal—and she hadn't even gotten a look yet!

Trusting that the hinges wouldn't squeak, she nudged the door wider and peeked inside. The bathroom was large and tiled in a slick white marble that reflected the moonlight beaming in from a skylight. No wonder there were no lights on. He hadn't needed them.

She could see everything.

His clothes made an uncharacteristically messy trail across the floor, as if he'd shed them in a hurry. The ancient hooded sweatshirt. Socks, sneakers. A crumpled red bandanna and a limp basketball jersey. Jeans. White cotton briefs.

The tub was filled to the brim, but the whirlpool jets weren't turned on. The water was perfectly calm and clear, very hot, judging by the steam that hung in the air. Five feet and ten inches of presumably naked man were sunk into it up to the armpits.

Adam had his eyes closed.

At first, Julia didn't move. Her gaze wandered over Adam's face. He looked peaceful, more relaxed than she'd seen him since his return. *Zen men,* she thought. *Gotta love them.*

Loath to disturb him but drawn nonetheless, she inched closer, stepping on his clothes so her boot heels wouldn't click against the hard marble. Adam didn't move—not so much as an eyelash. His arms were resting on the ledge of the tub, left hand dangling against the porcelain surround. Either he was in very deep meditation or he was asleep. Probably the latter. She should wake him up before his bones boiled down to jelly. Yes, indeed, she should. *Soon as she got a good, long look.*

His face made her stomach flip, so she let her gaze drift lower. Disappointing, that. All she could really see was his shoulders and the top of his chest. He had a nice clavicle, at least. Well defined. The rest of him was immersed, and though the water was clear, it was distorting, making parts of him appear to float...but not the parts that should float. Although the room wasn't fully illuminated, it was bright enough for her tell he was naked right down to his toes even if she couldn't discern details, just interestingly shadowy shapes. The thought of all that exposed skin—wet, warm and male—made her fingers twitch. What would happen if she touched him? Very, very lightly?

She leaned over the tub, one hand extended, one finger unfurling.

"What are you looking for?"

She froze. Then slowly, slowly turned her face toward Adam's, crystal shards prickling in her blood.

His eyes were open. Electric. Suddenly he surged upward in a spout of bathwater. She sprang back, but he'd already captured her, his fingers locked around her wrist. After the first wrench, she didn't try to escape. Why run when all she really wanted was to stay?

His quiet question hung in the air. *What are you looking for?*

"You," she said. *For the past ten years.*

"Fair enough." He released her and settled into the tub, propped higher this time. "You found me."

His wet chest had rippled with the motion, snaring her attention. He was lean as a greyhound, each sculpted muscle delineated against his bone structure like an anatomy illustration. She could see his ribs, which made her think of Cathy fattening up her new husband. Adam needed a woman to care for him—

Julia cut off the thought, squelching all domesticating instincts.

Adam wasn't looking for comfort. And she certainly didn't need to start thinking in those terms when she'd claimed to want the opposite.

"You found me. Now what are you going to do with me?" he asked, resting his head against the marble tiles but continuing to watch her, his eyes a prescient green, lit from inside, it seemed. She would have thought him relaxed if not for those eyes.

Her glance skimmed the water. His body was pale beneath it, tinged blue by the water, shadowed by the shifting moonlight. He did not move except to say in a deceptively mild tone, "Looking for scars?"

She blinked. Her voice came out sounding like a bullfrog. "No."

"Then why the inspection?"

"You're nude, Adam."

"I usually do that when I'm bathing."

"Yeah." She smiled. "So do I."

His brows went up. "Want to join me?"

She rubbed her wrist, still feeling the shock of his touch. "I think, um, I really think that I—"

"Don't think. Just answer."

"Are you injured?" she asked, so fast she clipped his last word.

"Where'd you get that idea?" He moved slightly in the cooling bathwater, poking one knee higher, spreading ripples across the surface. Every movement of his body fascinated her.

"From Zack. He stopped by to pick up Cathy when I was leaving. He mentioned—"

Adam scowled. "My nursemaid."

"You've been using the whirlpool regularly?" she guessed.

"It helps. Eases the aches and pains. But I'm not injured." He leaned sideways, extending an arm to her. "C'mere. I can prove it."

She stepped to the side. "You don't have to prove anything. I came only to, uh, check on you." Her hand waved carelessly. "Go back to your—your meditation."

He smiled a little, then sank back and closed his eyes. The water grew still. His breathing deepened and slowed.

The longest minutes of Julia's life ticked away inside her head. Again, Adam wasn't moving even an eyelash. How did he do that so easily when she was a bundle of nerves?

Another minute passed.

Well. She hadn't expected him to ignore her, but since he was...

His hand shot out and caught her wrist again. He held her tightly this time, pulling her closer so they were face-to-face. The heat of the bath made her flush; the heat of his eyes melted every thought inside her head.

"You were looking for scars," he said. "Should I stand for inspection? Let you see exactly how damaged the goods are?"

"Adam, you dolt. I wasn't looking for scars!"

He didn't respond, but the fierce stare was unwavering. He didn't believe her. She gazed into his hard, glittering eyes, realizing that beneath the tough-man act, he truly was feeling self-conscious, that it wasn't only wounded pride over losing his physical skills.

Of course, of course, she thought. He hid it well, but the accident had shattered his ego in all regards. Even with someone as confident as Adam, it would take a while to put it back together again.

"I was looking at you," she blurted. The flush spread up to her hairline, down into her collar. Even her ears felt hot. "I was—" She stopped and licked her lips, aware that her voice had dropped to a husky, sexy-sounding whisper. "I was admiring your body."

He said, "Oh," but he didn't let go, so she sank to her knees beside the tub and levered her hand onto his chest, thinking that he would certainly release her then. But he didn't. She stroked the firm pectoral muscle, and his arm moved with hers, his grip relaxing only slightly.

"It's a beautiful body." Her fingers slipped over his moist satin skin in a slow dance of sensation, bound only by the manacle around her wrist. "Let me go," she whispered, sliding a fingertip around and around his beaded nipple.

His lashes had dropped, making his eyes seem deceptively slumberous. "You need to stay right here."

"I will. I promise." She stroked his nipple, grazing it with a polished thumbnail.

He inhaled through gritted teeth.

Flick.

His grip on her wrist tightened. She pressed with her fingertip, eliciting a low moan.

The starting temperature of the water must have been near the boiling point, because it was still steaming. Strands of Julia's hair stuck to her cheeks and forehead. Moisture was collecting on her upper lip, trickling along the sides of her neck, pooling between her breasts. Inside, she was fomenting. The notion of stripping off every item of her clothing wouldn't go away.

"Release me," she coaxed, rolling the tight nub.

"No." Adam caught her other hand, threading his fingers through hers, and used it to draw her toward his mouth.

"I'm going to fall into the water."

"I'll catch you."

She held his gaze for the instant before the kiss. "You already have."

Their lips touched, warm and moist. There was tenderness—perhaps love—in the soft, caressing motions as they played together, making languid forays with their tongues. Kittenish purrs mixed with playful growls and mutual, soft laughter.

Eventually Adam let go of Julia's hands so he could clasp her head, his restless fingers stirring her sleek bob into disarray. In a swift rush of pleasure, their kisses deepened into hard, driving suction and thrust. She laid her palms flat on his chest, the ledge of the tub pressing into her hipbones as she let her weight rest fully on him so she could focus only on their kiss. Deeper, stronger. More and more and more.

They broke only to breathe. She rested her cheek against his, gulping in mouthfuls of humid air. "You're getting wet," he said, before finding her mouth again.

She nipped at his bottom lip. Her belly rubbed against the slick porcelain. "I certainly am."

He stroked a hand across her upthrust derriere. "Your jacket."

"Right." She went on her knees and ripped it off, past caring that the suede was patched with wet spots.

He tugged, undoing the collar of her blouse. "Take this off, too."

She stared at him from beneath her damp, clinging bangs. "You're sure?" she asked, not stopping for an answer as she yanked at the rest of the pearl buttons.

"Now I am." His eyes darkened at the sight of her white lace bra, a racy low-cut model that showed off every inch of what she considered to be a modest but adequate cleavage.

"How about..." She slipped the straps off her shoulders, letting them hang loose. "More?"

"Let me," he said, beckoning, his hot hand sliding to her waist. She leaned her forearms against his shoulders and bent over him, her breasts barely contained by the flimsy lace cups. Inside, she simmered with desire.

He slid lower into the water, the movement causing so much sloshing her bra turned transparent. Her nipples felt hard enough to cut through fabric even before he started licking at them with his tongue, abrading the ultrasensitive tips against the wet lace. "Take it off," she pleaded. "Quick."

He chuckled. "You always were a follow-the-proper-order girl," he said, using one fingertip to gently peel away the clinging lace.

The nakedness didn't quell her surging needs. She wanted his mouth on her, suckling away the ache. "Not anymore," she said. Water splashed over both of them as she threw herself into the bath, landing atop Adam's chest with a smack of wet skin. All but her legs were in the tub now, and those flailed, her boots kicking in the air as she grabbed Adam and plied him with enthusiastic kisses.

"Didn't you just say you take off your clothes to bathe?" he teased.

"You're a bad influence."

His brows went up. "Don't blame this on me. I followed protocol and stripped down first."

"Did you? I'd better check." She slid a hand down the center of his chest, plunging below the waterline to find the erection that had risen, hot and hard, against his groin. She caressed him boldly, marveling at the wet-velvet texture of his skin, the power pulsing beneath her palm. "Mm," she breathed. "Is this what they mean by up periscope?"

With a groan, he dropped his head back against the tiles. "That does it. Take off the jeans. You can keep your boots on if you want to."

As her jeans were wet to the thighs, she had to sit on the edge of the tub to wiggle out of them. Adam slid closer to help her, but his hands gravitated to her breasts instead, cupping them from behind. Julia nearly swooned at his touch. "I am so glad you talked to Zack," she said with a careless jubilance, struggling to shuck the jeans.

Adam's face was pressed near her spine, his tongue catching trickles off the edge of her shoulder blade; she didn't particularly expect him to respond.

"It's not that we needed permission, but all the same, it's a relief to..." Something stopped her. Maybe the silence. Maybe the sudden crackling tension. Maybe the cessation of Adam's electrifying hands and mouth.

She cocked her head. "You did talk?"

The stubble on his jaw scraped her back. "Yeah. We talked."

Exhale. "Good."

"Zack knows you're coming for Thanksgiving."

The steam had dissipated, but the air was still heavy and dank.

"As your date?" she prompted.

Adam murmured assent.

Julia crossed her arms over her breasts. "It's a start, I guess." Ever since the wedding, they'd been circling each other in fits and starts, gradually drawing nearer. Now it was as if their attraction was exerting a gravitational pull. Set them close enough and they came together in a fiery explosion, instant passion overwhelming reason.

In his prickly porcupine way, Adam was as principled as Zack. If she made love with him too soon, before the issues with his brother were resolved, they might find themselves right back where they started. Guilty coconspirators. It wouldn't matter to Adam how right and good and strong their relationship was. He'd focus on his betrayal of Zack, exactly the way he'd done before.

For him, the pattern was set in stone. Zack was the good son. Adam was the bad one. Good, bad. Right, wrong.

Which category was she?

"Did you tell him about..." She swallowed. "What happened? Ten years ago?"

"Not yet."

"If you don't, I will. I won't be a guilty secret this time around." Julia slid off the edge of the tub to the floor, her legs akimbo. The sodden jeans were tangled around her ankles, but she still wore her panties.

Adam put his arms around her shoulders. "Goldie?"

She'd never felt more exposed. "I don't want to do this."

"Why not?"

"You tell me. Up till now, it's been you stopping. I don't see how suddenly an invitation to a holiday dinner makes a difference."

"It doesn't. But your nude body does."

"So this is only lust?"

He hesitated. "Mutual lust, I thought."

"What about your principles regarding Zack? Wouldn't making love to me be repeating an old mistake?"

Water swirled as Adam withdrew. Suddenly the porcelain tub surround was cold against her spine, and she shuddered, not turning to look even when he said tiredly, "You were right. It was such a long time ago. Water under the bridge."

She didn't believe him. If their relationship wasn't to be illicit, having Zack's blessing mattered—immensely. Adam had allowed himself to be momentarily distracted from that, was all. Afterward, he'd tear himself up. She refused to be the friction that wore away at the brothers bond.

And how would that happen? a part of her wondered. *Are you clinging to the misbegotten notion that you two will be together long-term? Don't tell me you've forgotten that Adam's not a keeper.*

By his own definition.

"You're only saying that because sex is temporarily blinding you." Julia drew up her knees and dropped her forehead against them. Tightened her crisscrossed arms and tried not to sniffle.

"My control is better than that."

Which meant...? She hunched her shoulders. Droplets sprinkled over them as Adam rose from the tub, reaching for one of the luxurious for-show-only bath towels.

"I knew exactly what I was doing," he said. "But I can also take no for an answer." Out of the corner of her eye, she saw that he did have scars. She lifted her face. A raised pink line coiled around his left knee. A short, thick keloid marked the spot where a tree branch had gashed his opposite thigh. He'd had spinal surgery, she knew, so there must be others, hidden beneath the towel wrapped around his hips. Her heart clenched, but she didn't let the sympathy show in her expression.

Nor her unabated desire. The scars didn't hurt his appearance one bit. Looking at the man was enough to curl her damp hair into ringlets but, going by his brisk movements as he stepped into his jeans and tossed the towel away, they were having none of that. She was back in the good-girl category, by her own volition.

With a sigh, she turned and fished her bra out of the bathtub. Would they ever get their timing right?

THE PHONE WAS RINGING when Julia got home. She picked up just before the answering machine.

"Oh! Julia!" Cathy laughed. "I was expecting the machine."

"Just got home."

"So I guess that means it didn't go well?"

"It was—" Julia swallowed her response so fast her teeth clicked. "Um, what do you mean?"

Cathy chuckled. "You went to find Adam. Don't bother denying it. Zack and I figured it out about three seconds after you peeled rubber on Central Street."

Julia's stomach went hollow. She slumped sideways onto the overstuffed chair, her legs slung over the padded arm. "How much does Zack know?"

"Only what's obvious. You and Adam have the hots for each other."

No denying that. "And that's all he knows?"

"He's not thinking too deeply these days. There's very little blood getting to his brain."

Another reprieve. "Ah. A good old-fashioned case of honeymoon priapism."

"Pria-whatism?"

"Constant arousal."

"I see. Hmm. What's it called for women?"

"Probably nothing. Men wouldn't consider it a condition in need of medical attention." They laughed.

Julia shifted in the chair. Her backside was still damp. "You didn't call to brag about your devoted husband...."

"Nope. I was going to confirm Thanksgiving with you, but that was a ploy so you'd get back to me." Cathy's voice lowered. "It's the *secret*. I don't know if I can keep it from Zack, you know? When we first met, I was hiding my identity from him, and I regretted starting out on a lie. We've promised to be honest with each other. Even though this is your's and Adam's secret, knowing it and not telling Zack is making me feel sneaky."

Julia nodded into the phone, unable to speak through her clogged throat. "Ahem. Now you know how I feel. And why I had to break up with Zack."

"Can you imagine how it is for Adam?"

"He will tell." Julia swallowed. "I'm sure of it."

"He'd better do it fast. I can't take this, being an accessory to the, ah, to the—"

"To the crime," Julia said with a sigh. For all his running, Adam was locked up tight as a prison inside. Her, too.

"Zack's benevolent," Cathy said. "He'll understand."

Julia murmured agreement. She didn't doubt Zack's understanding. It was persuading Adam to believe in his own worthiness that was tough. Once he did...

They could be together at last. And together they would truly fly.

Mercilessly, she played on Cathy's giving nature to persuade her to hold out for a few more days, then hung up the phone and rose, staring out the window at the shadowed ravine, wondering if she'd be able to sleep. Vigorous exercise was not acting as the soporific it normally would. She was too keyed up sexually to find easy rest. This evening had proved that even the Zen man was restless and losing his control.

Something's gotta give.

Was it too much to ask that it be Adam, for once?

As she turned to leave the room, her glance fell on the white armchair. Indigo dye from her damp jeans had lightly stained the slipcovered seat in counterpoint to Adam's dirt smudge. There had to be symbolism in that, but she was too confused to decipher the meaning.

BENNY AND BONNIE KNOX weren't traditionalists when it came to holidays versus their jones for junk. Most of Julia's birthdays had been spent on the road, where she was lucky to get a cellophane-packaged cupcake with a candle stuck in it.

Thanksgiving weekend, they'd made plans to head south to Owensboro, Tennessee, for the twenty-third annual Bargain Bazaar of Crafts and Collectibles, working the show as both vendors and buyers. Julia had declined an invitation to come along, but she'd promised to stop by the antique emporium with turkey sandwiches when they returned in triumph with a load of goods to unpack.

The Brody Thanksgiving, on the other hand, was a slice of pure Americana. Football games blared on the TV in the den, where most of the men had gathered. The women clogged the kitchen, arguing about stuffing ingredients while covertly eyeing each other's dinner contributions—macaroni salad, Jell-O salad, marshmallow-topped sweet potatoes, four kinds of pie. Aunt Delilah sat with Emmie Marvin and the librarian, Cora Selverstone, giving directions to Cathy, the new wife, on how to set a proper table. Children ran around the house and in and out the doors, playing the traditional Thanksgiving game of Star Raiders, until finally they were called to take their places at the kids' table. Raising a chorus of the requisite oohs and aahs, Zack carried in the twenty-five-pound turkey. Reuben led the blessing. Then, while the side dishes began their journeys around the table, passed hand to hand, he carved the roasted bird.

The others fed their faces. Julia believed, New Ageish though it sounded, that she was feeding her soul.

She wanted this.

And Adam did not.

Should push come to shove and she could only have one, she'd choose Adam. If he let her.

Which was not to say that he didn't fit in. He talked football with the guys, was patient and kind with the elderly ladies, charmed the teenage girls with his sly grin and rapscallion ways and won over the middle-aged kitchen brigade with a well-timed double scoop of an unfortunate tofu-and-beet-juice mold Cousin Morgan had named beetofu. The kids loved him, too. He spotted while they climbed the willow tree, officiated a Star Raiders laser-tag fight and let the lone teenage boy take his prized mountain bike for a ride around the neighborhood.

But Julia wasn't convinced. She saw his eyes when he looked at the river and knew that he'd rather be launching a kayak than six-year-old Patti Brody's wood-bark boat. When he laughed at Uncle Brady's off-color jokes, his mind wasn't on what the stewardess said to the pilot—it was on jumping from the plane.

She wouldn't change that about Adam even if she could. So the only option was to join him. Give up her need for security and follow him to mountain, river, ocean, rock. Truthfully, the idea engaged her as much as it scared her. She wondered if she'd known all along that her rock-climbing lessons were only preparation.

Maybe, she thought, catching Adam's eye over the gigantic serving bowl of mashed potatoes. This time, when he looked at her, he really, truly looked at her.

When dinner was over, Zack shooed the older generation of Brody women out of the kitchen, saying that they'd done their share. His team would take care of the cleanup.

By the time the last lady had patted Zack's cheek, told his young wife what a prize she'd won and departed, Cathy was gagging behind a dishtowel. "Oh, please. You are such a suck-up, Zack Brody." She shared an exasperated look with Julia. "Why is it that men get so much credit for doing one-tenth of the household chores?"

"Because otherwise they'd do one-twentieth?" Zack guessed.

"Hmmph. Our children are going to be raised democratically. The boys will have as many household chores as the girls."

"Sure," Zack said. "The girls will also be doing an equal share of the yard work. Mowing the lawn, hauling the trash, washing the car..." He looked at Cathy and grinned, his eyes lighting up. She laughed, leaning in to his chest and murmuring words that were meant for him alone.

Julia looked away. She knew what they were referring to. Zack and Cathy had met over a sudsy car and a live-wire water hose. Good, clean fun, an appropriate situation for two such upstanding citizens. Julia and the Heartbroken gang had watched it happen before their very eyes.

Adam came in with the turkey carcass. "What's going on?"

"Your brother and sister-in-law are having a newlywed moment," Julia said.

Adam narrowed his eyes. "Hey. No sex stuff allowed in the kitchen."

Cathy looked at Zack and blushed bright red, guilt written all over her face.

"Don't tell me," Adam said, pretending horror. "I don't want to know."

"Yeah, he's strictly an au naturel kind of guy," Julia said as an aside, scraping plates into the garbage disposal.

"Who?"

"You, of course. *Zack* is civilized."

"Since when is sex in the kitchen more civilized than doin' it in the great outdoors?"

Zack scowled. "Shut up, Adam. I can still get the better of you."

"In the kitchen, maybe...loverboy."

Zack swung at Adam, who ducked low and went for his brother's midsection, wrestling him against the refrigerator. "You always were a secretive little weasel," Zack complained.

"And you were always too straightforward to understand the value of a good sneak attack." Adam stood upright, his face changing expression even before the words were all the way out of his mouth.

Julia knew what he was thinking. And by the look on Cathy's face, so did she. Of one accord, they threw down their sponges and left the room.

"WHAT WAS THAT ABOUT?" Zack returned to his station at the sink. "Girls?" he called. "We've still got dishes to do."

Cathy's voice carried past the closed door. "Put some of your muscles to good use for a change."

"For a *change?*" Zack called. He looked at Adam. "Do you believe that? Can't even get respect from my own wife."

Adam took a breath. The room was closing in on him. He'd been slightly claustrophobic ever since he was a little kid, when he'd climbed into a toy box and the lid had shut after him. It was one of his first memories—the black, the silence, the tightness that had pressed closer and closer upon him until he thought he'd stopped breathing altogether. Zack had found him, of course.

He shook the memory away. "That was a not-so-subtle hint."

Zack dipped a sudsy plate in rinse water. Most of the dishes had gone into the dishwasher, but their mother was particular about her fine china. "Too subtle for me, I guess." He handed the plate to his brother.

"We're supposed to have a heart-to-heart talk and make everything all right."

"I didn't know we were wrong."

There was a long silence before Adam spoke. "It's about me and Julia."

Zack shrugged and kept washing dishes. "You think I don't know what's going on between you two? Hell, the whole town knows."

"Uh, they do?"

"You know how they talk."

Adam cleared his throat. "This is more than that."

"This? That?" Zack turned, propping one wet hand on the edge of the sink, the other on his waist. "Why don't you just come right out with it?"

Adam reached through the thick, cottony air and laid the china plate on the counter. "Julia and I—we've been attracted to each for longer than you think."

"How long?"

He breathed, getting no oxygen. "More than ten years."

"Ten years."

"Yeah," Adam said softly.

"I see." Zack exhaled as he turned to face the sink. He

tilted his head back, making mental calculations. "Ten years. When Julia and I were still a couple?"

"Yes."

"Damn. I didn't see that one coming." He swung around to look at Adam. "When Julia called it quits with me, she admitted there was another man. Was it you?"

Adam nodded.

"But you weren't even around then. You'd taken off on a long trip that summer. To Montana, right? Even when Julia and I went away to college together, you still hadn't come home." Zack stopped. "Ah, I see. That's *why* you left."

"Sort of."

Zack didn't seem angry as much as confused. Absently he rubbed the end of his nose, as if he were piecing the memories together. "The way I see it, you and Julia have had nearly a decade to get together if you wanted to. What's the holdup?"

"Me, I guess. And you."

"You thought I'd be mad? Or jealous? Look, Julia and I are just friends—that's all we've been for years."

"It's not that," Adam admitted. "It's...my guilty conscience."

"It's been ten years. Time to get over it." Zack laughed. "I can completely understand how you'd be interested in Julia. She's a great—"

"It went further than that," Adam interrupted. "We went further." His throat closed. There. It was out.

He watched as the realization came over Zack's face. "You're saying that Julia cheated on me. With my own brother."

Adam's features wrenched. The truth was ugly—so ugly.

"It happened only once," he said. As if that made it any better. "Then I left town."

"That was why you went away so abruptly."

"Yeah. I thought you and Julia might be okay if I wasn't around."

Zack shook his head. "Not Julia—she wouldn't participate in a relationship that was only a charade." He gave an odd laugh. "At least not once it was made *that* clear."

"I'm sorry."

Anger tinted Zack's reproach. "You should have told me sooner."

Adam swallowed. Still no oxygen. "I know. I was a coward." And he was unworthy. He would not ask for forgiveness.

Zack turned away. "Damn. This is a shock. I have to absorb it, but I can't quite get my brain around the idea of you and Julia—" He winced. "Jeez, I must have been blind!"

"I'm sorry," Adam repeated. He felt cruel and useless, but he couldn't think of anything else to say.

Zack shot a look at his brother, as visceral as a hard, glancing blow. "Can you give me a minute? I accept your apology, all right? Maybe I can even understand why you did it. I just need a little time to adjust to the idea of—" He gestured in amazement.

"Yeah, sure, whatever." Adam backed away, groping for the door. The disappointment in Zack's eyes was killing him. He had to get away from it. "Sorry," he repeated. "Sorry." *Sorry, sorry, sorry.* It was the word he'd been waiting to say to his brother for all these years...and it wasn't near enough.

ON THE OTHER SIDE of the swinging door, positioned to guard the kitchen from interlopers, Cathy and Julia had overheard the entire conversation. They both had tears in their eyes but were trying not to look at each other lest they burst into blubbering sobs.

When she heard the bang of the back door, Julia slammed her eyes shut. Her heart sank, even though she'd expected this. Adam was gone. Possibly even for good; she couldn't know for sure.

"It'll be okay," Cathy said. "Zack will forgive him."

"And me?"

"Of course. You, too."

Her face screwed into a knot of misery; the unshed tears stung her eyelids. "I don't know if that's going to help."

8

HE BREATHED hot in her ear. "Are you sure this is what you want?"

She managed a nod.

"Tell me," he said, gripping her tightly.

"Yes." She rocked against his erection, aching to feel him inside her. This is my choice. "You, Adam. I want you."

The muscles in his lean back flexed beneath her hands as he lowered his head and opened his mouth over her breast and sucked on her flesh so that she felt the intense pleasure of it clear down to her toes. His hands were on her, too, jolts of awareness leaping from nerve ending to nerve ending wherever his fingers traveled, like small electric shocks. She opened her legs for him without a moment's hesitancy, inviting—no, asking him to take her. Now.

He said it, his voice soft and smoky with desire. "Now." And then he was pressing inside her, and she was gasping at the sweet pressure and instant of pain, her body twisting away from him with an instinctive flinch.

Adam stopped, poised over her, shuddering with tension. "Julia? You're not—"

She relaxed. Brushed her fingertips over his face. "It's all right. I want you to."

He shook his head as if dazed. The delay was unbearable to her. She moved against him, pressing a foot to the back of his thigh. "Go on. It's right. It feels—" she moaned as slowly, slowly he sank deeper "—so right."

He said, "I can't believe this is happening," and then he took her mouth in a deep, hungry, feasting kiss.

"JUST ONCE, I wish you'd come to me," Julia said from the shelter of the tall pine trees. Adam had sat in silence, listening as she'd parked her car, then walked around the development calling his name. The forest had been thinned to improve the view of the lake, so it hadn't taken her long to spot the flicker of his small fire by the shore. It figured he'd be roughing it outdoors, even though the temperature couldn't be more than forty degrees Fahrenheit.

She picked her way down the slope, stepping over the gnarled roots that crisscrossed the dirt like veins. "Just once," she repeated. "It would make for a nice change."

"I did come to you once," Adam said. "Remember?" With a snap, he broke a stick in half and tossed the pieces into the fire. "You weren't expecting me. And it didn't turn out so well."

"That depends."

"On your viewpoint?" He laughed bitterly. "Go ask Zack what he thinks."

"You left too soon. You should have stayed. I talked to Zack about it, tried to explain how it was. He's not angry with us—or at least he got over it fast. He knows we didn't intentionally set out to hurt him, and he said...he said—" She stopped, knowing every word out of her mouth sounded like a platitude. Adam didn't hide behind platitudes.

"I know," he said fiercely. "*Of course* Zack will forgive me. That's how he is. But..."

"It's forgiving yourself that's tough."

He shook his head. "Forgiving myself? Nope. That makes this all seem too simple."

Julia knelt by the fire, keeping her legs folded against her chest for warmth as she looked across the leaping flames at Adam's tortured face. "Explain it to me, then. Please."

He sighed, keeping quiet for so long she nearly gave up. But she'd learned patience in the past ten years, just as Adam had, and she intended to wait him out for as long as it took. They had to reach an understanding, because she couldn't take any more of this unsettled anguish.

He finally spoke. "It's not only you. It's Laurel, too."

Julia tucked her fists into her sleeves. She hadn't expected that, even though it made sense. The two brothers had shared Laurel—albeit more publicly—just as they'd shared her. The circumstances were different, yes, but not all *that* different. She should have seen before now that Adam needed to work both situations out with Zack. Possibly his feelings for Laurel were more complex than his feelings for her. *Their* one-night stand was old hat, by comparison.

Aw, hell, Julia thought. *This hurts.*

She kept her voice level. "What happened with Laurel—really? I only know that you two fought over her."

"Not the way you think."

She waited.

"It was my fault. I was seeing Laurel—"

Julia concentrated on his voice, ignoring the pain twisting in her gut.

"And she set it up to appear that she was also involved with Zack. I flew off the handle. Accused him of stealing my girl, basically. I guess that might have been a case of overcompensation for my guilt about doing the same to him." Adam stirred the fire, making the wood pop and crackle. "Anyway, we fought. Zack tried to warn me about Laurel and her lies, but I was just too damn bullheaded to listen."

"If you still wanted her, why did you leave?"

"You realize that at the time, none of this was so obvious. We didn't know about Laurel's ulterior motives. I guess I thought losing her to Zack was the punishment due me."

Julia shivered. "Then..." Her lips were numb, but it wasn't because of the chill in the air. "Then you still have *feelings* for Laurel? She could think of no worse punishment for herself than losing Adam to the most selfish and shallow woman in Quimby.

How could he *ever* have—

"I know what she is," he said. "Consider my interest in her temporary insanity."

Julia tilted her face to the sky. *Thank-you, God.*

"Was she pregnant? That was the rumor, you know."

Eventually Adam nodded. "I didn't find out about that until months later, when Zack was with me in Idaho during my recovery."

"Would you have married her, if you'd known?"

"You know I'm not as noble as Zack."

"I know no such thing. And that's not an answer."

"Okay, then—I don't know for sure what I'd've done, even if she'd given me the option. I'm sorry that Laurel lost the baby. Motherhood might have changed her for the better. But as far as marriage goes..." He winced. "No. I would have supported the baby, helped her raise it, but I don't think I could have married her. That would have been compounding the mistake."

The mistake, Julia thought. Great. She and Laurel were both check marks in Adam's big-mistake column.

She took a breath, the cold air stinging her lungs. "I don't understand why you were with Laurel in the first place."

Adam moved restlessly, rising to reach for a log. "Can't you guess?" he said when his back was turned as he searched the small woodpile he'd set to one side.

"No," she said, almost defiantly. There were times she swore she had no earthly idea of what went on in his mind.

He threw a log on the fire. Sparks rose like glittering fireworks. "C'mon, Goldie. It's obvious. On the surface, Laurel's the next best thing to having you."

Julia inhaled sharply. "How so? Should I be insulted?"

"I said on the surface."

"Laurel's all surface."

"She can be nice enough when she wants to be."

"That's true," Julia admitted. At one time, she'd counted Laurel Barnard as a friend. Not a close, trusted friend, but the kind of friends you are when you've grown up in a small town together, gone to the same schools, shared acquaintances and experiences and lunches and pom-poms. She'd made more allowances for Laurel's petty sniping than she ought to have, simply out of familiarity.

Adam groaned and stretched his muscles, raising his arms to the sky. She wondered how long he'd been sitting here in the cold. "There were two girls all the guys wanted when we were growing up," he said. "One was you, Goldie. The other was Laurel. The blonde and the brunette, the good and the bad. High-school boys aren't known for distinguishing between a nasty personality and a nice set of...legs."

She snorted. "Legs?"

"And other assorted parts."

"Weak excuse, Brody. You were well beyond teenage hormones when you got involved with Laurel."

"Do you remember how it happened? I'd stopped off for rest and recuperation after a six-day adventure race in Canada. The usual crowd went out on the town. You were there, wearing this little skirt with a zipper all the way up the center, and a see-through blouse—"

"That was the style at the time. I wore a sports bra underneath. Believe me, I was covered from armpit to armpit."

"Yeah, well, you were hot. Unbelievably hot. I couldn't take my eyes off you."

She looked at him, squinting against the veil of smoke. "What was Laurel wearing?"

He shrugged. "How would I know?"

She laughed, thinking, *Hmm.*

"We started playing Truth or Dare. Do you remember that?"

She nodded. She remembered, all right; she remembered him looking at her across the table. His hot gaze had made the crowd disappear. She'd thought that finally he was going to make his move on her.

"A question about first times came up. Naturally I didn't want to answer, so I took the dare instead."

"You always took the dare."

"And my dare was to French kiss the sexiest woman at the table."

"What a silly game."

"I couldn't kiss you."

"Why not?" She was remembering everything. It had been a Saturday night, and the group had been acting like sophomoric idiots, loud and noisy and laughing at the stupidest jokes. She'd sobered up pretty damn fast when Adam had taken the dare. With every cell in her body, she'd prayed that he would choose her. He'd stood up, started walking around the table toward her, she'd been melting with anticipation...and then he'd kissed Laurel. "Why didn't you kiss me?"

"Because kissing you wasn't a bar game. Kissing you was deadly serious."

She rocked closer to the flames. "I don't see what this has to do with you going off with Laurel."

"She didn't know she was second place with me. Or maybe I suited her plan to snare Zack, and she didn't care. Anyway, she, uh, came on to me pretty hard that night, and since I'd used up all my willpower staying away from you..."

Oh, great. He'd gone to bed with Laurel as a convenient substitute?

That was not flattering.

But it *was* proof. He'd never stopped wanting her, even though he was a typical male, distracted by every come-hither appeal aimed his way. It was like the joke. Why were men given penises? To make them easy to lead.

"Do you think we could stop talking about your ex-girlfriends now?"

"You were the one who wanted to know—"

She cut him off. "Yeah, sure. But enough's enough. Or I'll have to retaliate with ribald tales of briefcases and beepers."

"Is that the kind of guy you like?"

"It's the kind of guy who likes me."

"You sure?" Adam tilted his head sideways to look at her, and the mix of flirtation and devotion in his expression was just about the end of her. How much longer were they supposed to stay apart? Wasn't ten years enough penance?

"Is this finished?" she asked. "Can we quit rehashing the past now and just—" She stood and walked to Adam and put her arms around him. "Can we think about the future for a change?"

"I'm not good at that," he murmured, holding her, his face against her hair. His lips moved to her forehead, dropping small, soft kisses over her upturned face.

"Then can we think about *right now?*"

"I've been telling myself not to touch you for so long, this doesn't seem—"

She reared back. "If you say *right,* I'm going push you into the lake."

He drew her toward him again, moving his body against hers so she could feel the heat of his breath, the need in his voice, the quickening of his arousal. "Go ahead. I could use a cold bath right about now."

"If I can get you someplace where it's warm, I have other plans for you." She ran her palms down his jacket. To his jeans. To his fly. The growing bulge beneath it. Maybe she should grab hold and *lead* him inside.

"It's hot enough right where we are."

"It's freezing, Adam."

He flicked her earlobe. "You sure?"

She shivered. "I'm sure."

"'Cause it's warmer than that in here," he said, sliding his hand under her jacket. Her rib-knit sweater rucked up as he pushed higher, finding her breasts, touching them, teasing them—

Oh, my!

"Don't do that unless you're serious," she said, returning her hand to his fly.

He inhaled. "You, too."

"I'm seri—ah..."

He swept her into a deep kiss, his mouth opening on hers and sucking her into a world of heat and shuddering sensation. By the time he was finished, she was seriously drenched head to toe in hot, moist, steamy sweat, and damn what the thermometers read.

"You should hire yourself out to Triple A Heating and Cooling," she said, dazed. "Whew. Talk about running hot and cold."

His hands moved beneath her clothing. Her head lolled. Even her eyeballs seemed to swim in their sockets.

"Set of legs, huh?" she said, smiling with her eyes closed as he pushed aside her bra and closed his hands over her breasts. The play of his callused fingertips against her nipples was dizzying. Darkly erotic. Hot as blazes.

"You have great legs," he said, laughing against her cheek. Her arms were wound around his shoulders. She moved them to his neck, gripping tighter, turning her face so she could bite soft, hungry kisses at his cheek and jaw until she reached his mouth.

His hands were amazing. Gentle, rough, groping, skilled. Making her go a little bit crazy. "And you have great feet," she said between kisses.

"I like your elbows."

"Your chin."

"Shoulder blades."

Wrong side, she thought, a delicious lightness bubbling inside her. She rubbed against him. "Unfortunately..."

He raised questioning brows.

She frowned, moving her hips experimentally, testing the degree of his arousal. "Unfortunately, I'm afraid that your nose is just too darn big. All out of proportion."

"Good, because that's not my nose."

"Well, I hate to break it to you, but those aren't my shoulder blades, either."

"I didn't think so."

"Yes, you're quite an observant man."

"Are we going to do this?" he said, plucking at her mouth.

She shivered. *Are we? Finally? It seems too much to believe.* "Listen," she said, tilting her head.

He listened. Silence. The night was dark, cold, still. "I don't hear a thing."

"Right. That's the sound of nothing holding us back." One of his hands was still doing fantastic things inside her shirt, while his left arm had wound around her waist, his fingers dipping into the waistband of her woolen slacks. She snuggled against him, barely feeling the cold. His breath warmed her face. Each time the chill nipped at her nose or ears or chin, so did he. Warmed her right up.

"We could go to the show house," she said. "It's right up there."

"My sleeping bag's even closer. Next to the fire."

"But it's so—" *Oh, hell, why not?*

"C-c-cold?" There was a smile in his voice, even if she couldn't see it past her nose.

She kissed the smile. "Don't worry. I can take it."

"That's what I'm hoping."

Ah...

"Just don't think you're taking any of my clothes off," she warned as they moved toward the sleeping bag. He stopped. She pulled away, knelt and unzipped the quilted bag.

"Wait," he said. "I've changed my mind."

"Oh, no, you haven't. You're not allowed to." She kicked off her boots—luckily she'd worn thick socks—and hopped into the bag. It was cold, even with the fire nearby.

"The clothes part," Adam explained.

"They do," she said. "They part in all the crucial places. Thank heaven for buttons and zippers. We won't have to actually remove a thing."

His laugh echoed across the water.

She scrunched into the bag and patted the empty spot—a few spare inches—beside her. "Get in here."

The fire warmed and illuminated a small circle of space. The sleeping bag was positioned at the edge of it, where shadows gathered into dark. He sank to his knees and reached for her mouth, his exhale frosting the air. "Let's go inside," he said against her cold lips, "where it's warm." His mouth was warm on hers, licking, stroking. She parted her lips, sucked his tongue between them.

"No." She drew him down on top of her and managed to drag the zipper partway up. "I've never tried Popsicle sex before. Should be interesting."

"Should be *frigid,*" he said, but he was putting his hands inside her shirt again, sliding them to her breasts, and the heat leaped in her veins, leaped so high it chased away the cold. She didn't care that the ground was hard beneath her, that the space inside the sleeping bag was so tight they might as well have been making love in a mailbox, because this was Adam, at last she was with *Adam,* and that made everything right.

Made it perfect.

She tasted the hot sweetness of his mouth on hers, and it was an ambrosia of wild musk and hard male and whispered need. He splayed his fingers over her breasts, sending shivers—hot shivers—over her skin and deep into the heart of her. They rocked together, moving sensuously, their legs tangled and their mouths joined in frantic dancing lust.

After a time, Julia moaned in frustration. It was impossible to do all that she wanted. Adam was on top of her, holding her down and in and tight, giving her no opening to get her hands on him where she wanted—on his skin, his hot, sliding muscles, the hard thrusting erection that pressed between her thighs. She worked one arm up and wrapped her fingers around the collar of his jacket, practically biting through the denim when he shoved up her jacket and shirt and bra all in one motion and placed his open mouth over her breast so fast she barely registered the instant of cold exposure. He said *um,* and she said *oh,* and then he flicked his tongue and pulled hard on her nipple and she tilted her head against the hard-packed ground, seeing a flash of diamond-bright stars as her eyes rolled back in ecstasy.

She writhed against him, lost in the tormenting pressure and suckle of his mouth, his body heavy on top of her, the passion driving every sensation but pleasure out of her head. Her arms were trapped. All of her was caught, entangled, ensnared. She could do nothing but close her eyes and sink into the heat and desire, let it happen, let it go, let it come…

Oh, let it come.

Without taking his mouth away from her breast, Adam was able to lower the zipper of her pants and reach inside. Julia jumped under the touch, the flames inside her crackling into an inferno. His fingers grazed her belly, tracing tickling patterns upon her skin as he dragged away her panties, taking advantage of the arching pleasure that had lifted her hips off the ground. His palm slid across her skin, brushing between her thighs but not stopping. She let out a sob, needing to open her legs. "I can't," she said, trying to circle her hips, to turn the exquisite pressure inside her into motion before she died from the frustration.

"I can," he answered, releasing her for the few seconds it took for him to rip open a Mylar packet with his teeth and extract the condom. She kicked one leg free from her pants.

Adam reached down, moving heavily against her. "Is this too uncomfortable for you?"

"Uh-uh," she said.

"Too cold?"

Their body warmth had created a surprising coziness inside the sleeping bag. Her face was cold, but that was all. "I hear friction keeps a body warm," she said, rubbing against him, finally able to get one hand inside his clothing to stroke the skin stretched taut across his abs. He'd loosened his jeans, and she dipped lower, slipping her hand front to back and then lower yet, reaching for him as she wrapped her free leg around his hip and he laced his fingers through her hair, taking her mouth, biting at her lips while she guided him inside her, slowly inside her, where hot steel melded with glowing warmth.

There was a moment of acclimation and then he stroked in and out of her and she arched into the hot pleasure of it, sighing his name. He put his elbows near her shoulders, his hands still in her hair, and moved faster, faster, striking a hard, jolting rhythm, his body scraping roughly against hers everywhere but the point at which they met in wild slippery need.

Julia was feverish. Even the air seemed warm. The fire was a flickering beacon in the black night, casting Adam's face half in shadow, half in golden light as he leaned down to find her mouth in a crushing kiss that came at the exact moment that the tinder point was reached and her body burst into a series of fiery explosions.

She lay, gasping beneath his weight as he stroked her hair and inside her mouth and then deeply into her body, shuddering and breathing her name as he came. She hugged him tight, not letting him move away so she wouldn't lose the closeness and warmth and miracle of their lovemaking. "Thank you," he whispered, kissing her ear, her hair, his hands layering more heat on her exposed skin with reverent caresses that traveled from breast to hip and back again.

She smiled and said, still stunned, "Thank you for choosing me."

"I always chose you. I just couldn't have you."

She wanted to argue that they'd wasted a lot of years when they could have been together if only they'd dared, but it was too nice lying in his arms with her skin all tingly and the happiness inside her oozing out of her pores, maintaining the warmth. "That was something," she said. She could feel his heart pounding against hers. That really was worth waiting for.

He nuzzled into her hair, murmuring agreement.

"It might even have been perfect." Smiling, she closed her eyes. When Adam didn't respond, she nudged him. "You think?"

"Aside from the bumpy ground, the cold, the lack of light so I couldn't really *see* you—" He glanced down, moving against her with a wrench of their tangled clothing and the twisted enclosure.

She muffled her laugh in the flap of the sleeping bag. "Yeah, aside from that."

He kissed her. "It was perfect."

"THERE ARE no sheets on this bed," Adam said a few minutes later. If he knew anything, it was that Mother Nature was relentless. Their warming passion had lasted only so long before they became aware that maybe they were cold, after all. He'd reached around and touched Julia's bare bottom, and it had been like ice, so he'd zippered and buttoned her and hustled her up to the house.

"It's a show house," she said. "A facade." She looked under the comforter at the bare mattress. "In fact, I'm surprised there's even a mattress at all. It might have been just a cardboard box."

"And you expected me to sleep here?"

"Why not? You like roughing it." With a twinkle of her eyes, she brushed her fingertips across her abraded lip, then down to her breasts.

He grinned a little sheepishly. Next time, they'd do it slow and soft and easy. He'd take his time, get to know every inch of her, every taste of her all over again.

She shrugged. "It's not my fault if you made a poor bargain."

"As I remember it, it wasn't a bargain. It was a dare." He thought back to his first day in Quimby. "Tell me, Goldie—did you really want to defy death? Or was that just a ploy to get my attention?"

"Couldn't it be both?"

"I even wondered if you were in cahoots with Zack to get me back into shape."

"Don't mix me up with Laurel. I'm not *that* manipulative."

"I wasn't going to blame you. I was going to thank you."

"Oh."

"Thank you."

She crawled onto the bed on her knees, reaching over to put her arms around him. "I didn't do anything. You were already in pretty good shape. All you needed was a reason to get out there again."

He kissed the top of her head; her hair smelled like smoke. "Did it ever occur to you that if I'd quit climbing, I'd be more likely to stick around Quimby?"

"Not for even a moment," she said fiercely. Her embrace tightened. "If you wanted to quit, that would be one thing. But there's no way I'd hope for you to stop. Or especially try to convince you to stop."

"The danger doesn't scare you?"

"Of course it does."

"Then..."

She looked into his face. Gave his denim jacket a little tug. "Don't you remember? Danger is your middle name. I wouldn't know you if you weren't taking risks."

He didn't want to hurt her, but he knew he had to. He couldn't do it while he was touching her, so he moved away from the bed, his boots making scuff marks in the plush carpeting. All around him was the cold, perfect beauty of the professionally decorated bedroom—pristine pin tucks, precisely arranged folds, silk flowers that looked real but would never die. A facade, he thought. This type of perfection was only a facade.

Julia's questioning face was reflected in the mirror over the vanity. He stopped his restless pacing and looked at her. Julia—she was perfect. She was real. He loved her.

But that wasn't enough to keep him in Quimby for good.

He cleared his throat. "You know that sooner or later, I'm going to be moving on."

At first, the only sound she made was a whisper of an exhale. Then she said, "I know," and bowed her head. She sank lower onto the bed, her legs folded beneath her. Her chest hitched, but her voice stayed level, even casual. "I'm betting on sooner rather than later. I know nothing's changed."

Everything's changed. Anguish ripped into him, swift and strong. He gripped the edge of the vanity to keep himself from faltering. *Damn.* He hadn't expected to feel such pain at the thought of leaving her. *I could ask her to come with me,* he thought, but that would be insane when he had no idea where he was going. Julia was settled in Quimby, with her lovely, clean house and her stable, secure business. She wasn't a pick-up-and-go girl.

It was impossible. She wouldn't go, and he couldn't stay, so all that was left for them was to enjoy the here and now until their time together ran out.

Why did that suddenly seem so bleak?

He looked at Julia, trying to be so brave. In another five years, he'd come back to find her married with children. Married to some really nice, really solid guy who'd know how lucky he was and would treat her like a queen, with all the devotion she deserved. She'd be happy. She'd be content. She'd still love Adam, he knew she would, but it would be with a certain fondness and distance, because she'd have gotten him out of her system at last.

He could live with that. Why not? It was what he wanted.

It was his choice.

9

SHE WAS PANTING. Her head twisted back and forth on the pillow. For an instant he mistook her expression for pain, but then she opened her honey-colored eyes and looked straight at him and he saw her heat and pleasure and need for more.

He thrust deeper. Her legs coiled around his. Her hands tightened on his shoulders, fingernails biting.

"Yes," she sighed, moving beneath him. All around him. Tight, liquid silk, hot as a furnace. He wasn't thinking, only reacting, driven by raw impulse to plunge even deeper into her, again and again, all emotion, no technique.

And she said "Yes!" again, crying out as she rose to meet his frantic pace.

JULIA'S STOREFRONT office was on Blemhuber Street, two over from Central. She had a part-time secretary and a couple of freelancers who paid a percentage to use Quimby Real Estate as a base of operations. It wasn't unusual for her to be the only person in the office. The secretary worked afternoons, after her morning job answering phones for the Church of Redeeming Virtues, and the freelancers were in and out all the time, sometimes showing houses, sometimes sleeping late. Julia wouldn't bet on the former. Neither had sold a house in two months. Which *might* have been because all Quimbyites came straight to her.

If I wasn't here...

Julia shook her head. Of course she'd be here. Where else?

Not with Adam. *Certainly* not with Adam.

Unless...

After a moment of thought, she smiled and got to work. It was already a good morning. She had two new listings.

LATER THAT WEEK, Adam stopped in at the Central Street Café to pick up lunch for him and Julia. He had big news, and she was the first person he wanted to tell.

In the days since they'd made love, she'd been so cheery about his leaving that he'd begun to feel kind of disgruntled. Yesterday, she'd even canceled the rest of their rock-climbing lessons. It was too cold now, she'd said. And he'd be leaving soon, anyway, so what was the use? He thought there might have been a little dig behind that comment, but, nope, she'd met his eyes straight-on and smiled as if waving him goodbye was just another item to check off her to-do list.

Well, hell, he'd thought at the time, tempted again to ask her to come along even though that was impractical. The new, daring Julia might have climbed a few rocks, but she was still the most practical, levelheaded person he knew. He wouldn't change that about her any more than *she'd* ask him to stop taking risks.

Considering the phone call he'd received this morning, he was relieved that he'd held his tongue. Leaving was going to be easier with Julia being so sensible about the inevitable.

She'd probably celebrate with him. All the same, he dreaded telling her. For his sake, she'd hide her distress, but the news was going to hit her hard even as she congratulated him.

He didn't bother picking up a menu. With little to choose from that wasn't deep-fried or covered with cheese, he placed an order for two salads with extra sprouts and dressing on the side, then asked for hot tea while he waited.

He was sitting at the far end of the counter with his tea when there was a flurry of activity at the door. A woman had come into the café and was holding the door closed against a person following behind her. "No, Franco, no! I can't have lunch with you." The door lurched partway open. She grabbed the handle and pushed it shut with all her strength. "Please go back home, Franco. Leave me alone!"

Everyone else in the room was laughing and shaking their heads, so Adam went to the door to give the lady a hand. "Can I help?" he said, and then stopped dead.

Laurel Barnard.

He hadn't recognized her at once because her long hair was cut so short it curled around her ears, but it was definitely Laurel, the woman who'd come between him and Zack, but only as a poor substitute for Julia. The shock of seeing her again made Adam wonder if he'd subconsciously *wanted* to force the truth into the open, and that was why he'd gone out with Laurel in the first place. After all, she'd been after Zack for as long as he could remember. He'd had no reason to believe she'd settle for him instead.

Laurel was equally startled, her green eyes widening when she glanced over her shoulder and saw him standing nearby. "Adam?" She stepped back, forgetting the door. It immediately swung open, and a short fellow burst through, red in the face and breathing hard. The black strands of his comb-over were floating above his fuzzy receding hairline like a broken spider web.

"Laurel, my *bellissima,*" he said, followed by a long string of sticky-sweet pet names that ended with him smooching on her cheek.

She pulled a face and batted at him. "Ew! Franco! Let me go!"

Adam blinked. "Is this your new boyfriend?"

Laurel made a sound of frustration and pushed the man away. "No, of course not."

'*Cara mia* has forgotten our long nights of passion aboard the *Sea Siren,*" said Laurel's Romeo. He looked to be in his forties, with the face of a has-been matinee idol. He was dressed in an expensive suit, which had clearly been custom-made to fit his squat frame. His upper body was well-developed, but his legs were so short the tailor must have cut an excess six inches of fabric off the bottoms of his trousers. "We sailed on an ocean of bliss, *ma bella.*"

"Ai caramba!" said the counter waitress, Philly somebody-or-other, who was leaning against the cash register, thoroughly enjoying the spectacle.

Laurel flung her head back, her nostrils flaring in outrage. "That's not true!" she wailed. "Why won't anyone *believe* me?"

Franco flung out his arms and smacked his lips. "Because they see the love in your eyes."

Adam stuck out his hand. "Adam Brody. Good to meet you." He'd been dreading his first encounter with Laurel, but this wasn't bad at all.

The dark little man grinned widely, showing big white teeth—probably caps. "Frankie Zook. I'm the Plumbing King of the Tri-State Area. Service and fixtures, the whole deal." Reaching for the handshake, he slapped a business card into Adam's hand. "You ever move to Jersey and need a new toilet, you call Frankie and I'll give you the best deal of your life."

"Huh?" Adam said, wondering what had happened to the Italian accent. The *bad* Italian, he realized, overdone like rubbery spaghetti.

Laurel rolled her eyes. "He's from New Jersey. We met on a cruise, and now I can't get rid of the fraud."

Frankie puffed out his chest. His midsection stayed inert, held in so tightly Adam suspected there was a truss involved. "Frankie Zook ain't no fraud. I have a castle, *bella,* just like I told you. Casa Plumbico. Three thousand square feet of showrooms. We got wall-to-wall, top-of-the-line porcelain, marble and fiberglass."

"Just think, hon," the waitress said to Laurel, snickering. "You marry Frankie, and you'll finally have that throne you've been wanting all your life."

Laurel glanced over the café, taking in the chuckling faces of the diners, all of whom seemed to be reveling in her predicament. She whipped around in time to catch Adam's grin. "Don't you laugh at me. Don't you dare—" She gritted her teeth and clenched her fists, quivering with frustration.

Adam made an attempt at a serious expression. His and Laurel's relationship had been no laughing matter. But it was just so perfect, seeing her get her comeuppance in the form of the Plumbing King of New Jersey. She'd always had delusions of grandeur.

"Bellissima," Frankie crooned. "I would never laugh at you. I lay my empire at your feet. Just say the word, and you will be my queen."

"Go for it," the waitress said, whipping up a chorus of yeahs and yahoos from the onlookers.

Laurel flushed. She glared at Philly, at Adam, then

made another pent-up screeching sound and tore out of the café, Frankie on her heels. The Plumbing King looked like a very determined man.

After the buzz had died down, Adam collected his take-out order from the waitress. "What was that about?"

"Poetic justice," Philly said as she rang up the bill. "A few days ago, Laurel came back from her cruise bragging about this Italian count she'd met named Franco, who was crazy for her. Then flowers and gifts began arriving. Imagine our delight when Frankie Zook showed up yesterday, looking to sweep Quimby's own little hoity-toity princess off her feet."

Adam smiled. "Definitely a case of be careful what you wish for."

Philly chortled. "Yeppers, you can say that again."

"YOU'LL NEVER believe it," Adam said when he got to Julia's office with the salads.

She hung up the phone. "I already heard. That was Gwen."

"I didn't see Gwen there."

"The waitress, Philly, told her."

"The grapevine in this town is amazing. But not infallible," he said, setting one of the salads on her desk blotter.

She lifted the lid. "Oh, good, extra sprouts. I can't tell you how much my mouth is watering." Belatedly, his words registered, and she looked up from the food. "What's that? Did something else happen with Laurel?"

Adam took one of her client chairs. "Isn't Frankie Zook enough?"

"I haven't had the pleasure yet, but it sounds like it."

She dumped all her blue-cheese dressing onto the salad at once. "What did you think of him?"

Adam stirred his salad with a plastic fork. "You know, it sounds crazy, but Laurel ought to give him a chance. It could be a match made in heaven. The Plumbing King thinks she's as much of a princess as she does. Where else is she going to get unconditional adoration?"

Julia chuckled. "You have a point."

They munched their greens. Adam started to speak a dozen times, but stopped. It was hard to find the right words.

"How did you feel about seeing Laurel again?"

His head went up. Julia was looking at him, blinking, every hair in place, every emotion in hand. "It was..." He paused. "It was okay. We didn't really talk, so we didn't argue. I thought I might be extremely uncomfortable, but all I felt was regret. She used me, but in a way I used her, too."

"How so?"

"It wasn't intentional." He paused, thinking how to explain. "Did you ever consider how that triangle was an echo of the one between you, me and Zack?"

Julia sucked in a breath. "You're right. The difference is that this time the, um, *deceit* was brought out in the open. It didn't fester."

Adam grimaced. "I let confessing my digressions to Zack become this gigantic obstacle in my mind."

"How's that been?"

He shrugged. "We're treading lightly around each other."

They returned to the salads. After a while, Julia stopped suddenly, mid-chew. Her finger went up while she finished the mouthful. "Wait a minute." She swallowed. "Was there something else you wanted to tell me?"

He almost smiled. That was Julia. A mind like a steel trap when it came to the little details. No threads left dangling.

"There was," he said.

Her head inclined. "Well?"

Up-front, he thought. *Like Julia.* "I've been invited to join a team of professional adventure racers. We'll train in Colorado for the next several months before our first race."

It was a few seconds before she responded. Carefully. "Adventure racers? I know about them. You've done those races before—they're the ones that take days and have you hiking up and down mountains and through jungles and deserts and—and..." She waved a hand.

"That's right. The different legs of the competition vary—biking, kayaking, climbing, swimming—hell, sometimes even caving."

"And they go on for miles and miles and days and days...."

"Yes."

She fixed him with her most direct gaze. "Is your body up to it?"

"It will be. I'm greatly improved. I don't need the cane anymore. I'll have to go slow at first—"

"Ha," she said. "Your idea of slow is a hundred miles on a bike before noon."

"I'll take care of myself, Goldie. Promise."

Her chin dimpled. Her voice got small. "You'll be traveling all over the world. These races are held in places like Morocco and Patagonia, aren't they?"

"Some of them are, yes."

There was a long silence.

"Well," she said, blinking, "imagine that. I've been taught to rock climb by one of the best. It's not every amateur that gets such a skilled teacher. Lucky me."

Her eyes were not so pleased. They were sad. He choked up. "You know what this time with you has meant to me."

"Sure. Me, too," she whispered. "When do you leave?"

"Soon enough."

She sank back in her chair and put her face in her hands. "I forgot to say congratulations." A beat. "Congratulations."

He couldn't respond.

"Your teammates must have a lot of faith in you. What a thrill to be chosen like that." She raised a bleak face that had been painted over with a smile. "Especially after the accident. I guess this means you've made a complete recovery."

He cleared his throat, but it didn't clear. "I'll find out when I begin serious training. There's no guarantee. I could get injured again and be replaced overnight."

"You won't be."

"*Everyone* gets injured in adventure racing."

"You're tough."

So are you.

"This isn't a permanent goodbye," he said, clutching at the thought the way he'd clutched to the side of a mountain and promised God he'd never take another risk. He could only hope the comparison wasn't too accurate. "Well see each other again. You can come—"

She held up a hand to silence him. He succumbed. This *was* goodbye, and she knew it. If only they'd had more time together, he thought, although that was just more foolish blather. One day or a hundred days, a week or a year—it wasn't enough. He needed her the way he needed the air he breathed. She was as vital as his legs, his muscles, his bone, his heart.

If I leave, I'm tearing out my heart.

And if I stay, I'm shutting it down.

Julia tossed back her head. Her face was naked—stripped to essentials. "You know what I want?"

"What?" he said, hoping he could grant her wish.

"I want you to make love to me. Right now. Right here." He hadn't expected that. She leaned forward, meeting his eyes. Hers were red around the rims, but she wasn't giving in to the grief.

Brave girl.

"Right on this desk with the phones ringing and clients banging on the door. I don't care about them. Just you." Her chin wobbled. "Can you do that for me?"

A familiar heat and a less familiar but just as strong desire to be her hero surged up in his veins. He found her in his arms so fast it was possible that he'd catapulted over the desk. He said, "Know that I love you," and then she was kissing him, making yearning sounds at the back of her throat, biting at his mouth and clawing at his shirt. He put his hands around her bottom and lifted her onto the desk, and she swept the salads and her neat piles of papers and files off it in one motion, sending them toppling and spilling and smearing in one hell of a mess. *Not Julia,* he thought, but then she stripped off her blouse and put his hands on her breasts and he thought, *Yes, Julia* as her roundness and warmth and sucking mouth enveloped him like a swelling ocean wave. *Yes, yes, yes, Julia.*

THE NEXT DAY, she was gone.

Adam went to her office first, only to find a middle-aged woman with a strong face and a white Julia-style bob, outfit and manicure sitting behind the desk and looking very pleased with herself. The surface was completely bare—not even Julia's stainless-steel desk lamp remained.

He stared rudely. "Where's Julia?"

"Good question." The woman barely glanced up; she was absorbed in swiveling her rear end in the rolling chair and stroking the silky wood desktop. "We'd all like to know."

"You must have some idea."

"Not really. She only said that she was leaving and that I should take her place."

"For how long?"

"As long as I want it."

He clenched his jaw. "How long will she be gone?"

The woman who was not Julia swore she didn't know. At least he had her attention now, even if her eyes narrowed with avaricious intent as she looked him over. "Say...are you in the market for a house?"

"No, only Julia," he said, and fled.

HE WENT straight to Scarborough Faire.

Cathy was up on a stepladder decorating trees for her Christmas displays. Strings of beads and a spiraled copper garland were wound around her neck like necklaces and a feather boa. The pocket of her apron was stuffed with glittery ornaments that had shed their glitter on her hands and sleeves. Despite the holiday attire, she looked at him with a sour expression when he asked her about Julia. "I didn't think you were so dumb, Adam."

"What does that mean? She seemed fine with me leaving. Didn't say a word against it."

Cathy stuck out her lower lip—there was glitter on it, too—and blew out a big breath. "Did it never occur to you to ask her to go along with you?" She sneezed into her cupped hands. Glitter flew everywhere.

Tiny sparkles floated onto Adam's face as he looked at his sister-in-law, unprepared for such a blunt question. "Uh, sure it did. But I knew that wouldn't work. Julia wouldn't—"

"Yes, she would. She'd go with you to Colorado. She'd go to Katmandu. Heck, it wouldn't surprise me if she'd even agree to climb to the top of Everest."

"I don't think so." He stepped back, brushing glitter off his face. "You think... Julia? No. She's not the type."

"The *type?*" Cathy rolled her eyes heavenward. "Don't you mean *typecast?*"

"I'm not doing that." He stopped, his brow wrinkling. "Am I?"

Cathy climbed off the stepladder and put a friendly hand on his shoulder. "Think about it. Julia might look like Ms. Conservative Businesswoman, but has she *ever* been that way with you?"

Flash images of her clicked through his mind's eye. Julia in the awful orange bridesmaid's dress, confronting him. Julia in the open cupola, the wind in her hair, Julia climbing rocks, repeating her mantra under her breath all the way up without even realizing it. Julia swinging down the cliffside on the rappel line, laughing with joy. Julia...jumping into his bath. Julia...making love to him inside the sleeping bag. And on her desktop. Without reserve.

Julia, eighteen years old. Kissing him, saying that it was him she wanted. Him, all along.

She'd given him her trust, her reputation, and most precious of all, her heart.

One risky move right after the other.

And *he'd* played it safe, always holding a piece of himself back. Expecting touch-me-not perfection from the golden girl of his fantasies, when Julia—the real level-headed, laughing, flawed, sexy Julia—was already everything he wanted.

"Where is she?" he asked Cathy, his voice rusty as old nails, making his mouth taste bitter and acidic.

"I honestly don't know." Cathy shrugged, glittering and jingling as she climbed up the stepladder. "But she did come to our house last night to talk to your brother."

Adam was surprised, even though he knew that Julia and Zack had stayed friends. Maybe he'd assumed that his confession had changed that. "About what?"

"I couldn't say." Cathy placed a golden glittery star at the top of the tree, not worried in the least. "If you want to know, you'd better go see Zack."

"THERE'S A FOR SALE SIGN planted outside Julia's house," Adam blurted as soon as he found Zack in the partially renovated barn that sat on the country acreage he and Cathy had recently purchased. Adam had stopped by the house on his way to Zack and had been twitchy inside ever since. Not like him at all. At least not the adult him. "She can't be serious."

Zack looked up from the house plans he'd spread over a makeshift drafting table, as solid and calm as ever. "Have you ever known Julia to make an impulsive move?"

Yes, Adam thought, filled to bursting with the epiphany Cathy had prompted. But now was not the time to get distracted. Before he got ahead of himself, he had to figure out what craziness Julia was up to.

"What do you know about it?" he demanded, seeing that Zack wasn't altogether surprised by the astonishing piece of news.

"I know nothing about her selling her house."

"But you do know something about something."

"Yes. Julia and I had a good talk last night. Before she left, she wanted to be sure that there were no hard feelings between us."

Adam's brain bounced between *a good talk* and *before she left,* not sure which to question first. He settled on saying, "Tell me everything."

"Why?"

"What do you mean, *why?*"

"You're leaving town again." Zack shrugged, but there was disappointment in his eyes. "You're leaving Julia behind, so what do you care what she does?"

"Jeez, not you, too." Adam whirled. He had to move. Restlessness was running through his body like a class-five rapids, making every feeling he'd ever had churn in its turbulence. "Of course I care what she does." He stopped, stared at the network of massive old rafters that had been sandblasted to fresh, honey-toned wood. The old nicks and scars remained, for character. "I love her," he said.

"Whatcha say?" Zack called. "I didn't hear you."

Adam took a deep breath. "I love her."

Zack shook his head. "Sorry, but that's not good enough."

Adam advanced on him. "Then what?"

Zack kept shaking his head. "I'm not going to push you into this one."

"You pushed me into walking again."

"I kicked you in the butt when you needed it. Not the same thing. You already *wanted* to walk."

"You think I don't want Julia?"

"Not enough."

Adam felt as though he was breathing fire. The loss of Julia burned in his veins. "You don't know what I feel."

"Maybe not, but I know that you told her you're leaving. Action speaks volumes."

Adam was disgruntled by his brother's complacency. "Do you have to be so damn steadfast all the time?"

"I've had a lot of practice, acting as your ballast." Zack gave a head bob. "Maybe you ought to stop worrying about what *I* think and start worrying about you and Julia."

Adam went still. "Does that mean you can accept me and Julia as a couple?"

The air became dense. The question had sucked all lightness out of it in one breath.

"I accepted it all along," Zack said. "I'd even hoped you two would get together. Of course, I didn't know that you already had—" he winced "—so it took me a few days to adjust my thinking. But now that I have..." He turned up a hand, offering it to his brother. "Don't let me stand in your way. Go after her, Adam. Let her know that you love her and want to be with her. I have a hunch that the details will work themselves out."

Adam silently replayed his brother's words. *Go after her.*

Then he thought of Julia, coming to him in the firelight. *"Just once I wish you'd come to me."*

He would do it, whether or not it was the smart or sensible choice. Maybe this one time would make up for all the other chances he'd had when he'd turned and walked away.

He went to Zack. They clasped hands in a brief, firm shake, giving a mutual mental shove to the boulder that had been blocking the way to forgiveness. The down slope was as steep and dangerous as it had always been. But when Adam inhaled, he believed for the first time that his guilty shame was gone for good.

His thoughts returned to Julia. "I want to try," he said. "But I have no idea where she's gone."

"Ah. Sorry. I can't help you there." Zack frowned. He rubbed two fingers along the side of his nose, then squeezed the tip—his usual thinking posture. "But I do know she's off—and these are *her* words—proving herself."

FEELING AS IF he'd been running around town like a chicken with its head cut off, Adam went back to Cathy's arts-and-crafts shop to beg, borrow or steal Julia's house key. She encouraged him on his quest, turning the key over without argument.

Once he let himself inside, there was nowhere to turn. He'd hoped to find a clue to Julia's whereabouts, but the house was so clean and spare there was nothing to go on. The bed was made. The closets seemed untouched, except for an empty space where she'd taken down a suitcase. There were no notes on the fridge or itineraries tucked away in the desk. Even the wastebaskets had been emptied.

He walked around the house, swearing with frustration. The only option he could think of was to turn on her computer and go through her files. An invasion of privacy, but he'd already done that by letting himself into her house.

He strode to the floor-to-ceiling windows and stared at the ravine. It was a stark and wintry view, a lifeless vista of ink scratches on white paper. The sky was a cloudless gray.

Proving herself, he thought. What did that mean? She wasn't dense like him. She wouldn't try to climb the Thornhill cliffs on her own. So what else was there? River rafting? Bungee jumping? Skydiving? Too cold.

He turned, intending to try the computer, and his glance fell on the big white armchair. The cushions were smudged. Odd that Julia hadn't attacked the stains with an upholstery cleaner. He moved closer and was distracted by the telephone on a table beside the chair.

The telephone. Of course.

He slid out the drawer and removed the phone book. Flipped it open to the travel agency listings, hoping one would be underlined or starred, but no such luck. There was always redial, but when he tried that he got Cathy saying, "Scarborough Faire. Cathy Brody speaking."

He asked her if she knew what travel agency Julia used.

"Sure. There's only one in Quimby. Travel A Go-Go. Gwen's mother runs it." Cathy chuckled. "She's as big a blabbermouth as Gwen. You won't have any trouble getting her to talk."

JULIA'S TEETH were chattering, and the plane hadn't even lifted off the ground yet. The engine was rumbling—she could feel it shaking the floor beneath her—but they hadn't moved. There were two other skydiving students in the plane besides her, and they both looked as wide-eyed and nervous as she felt. Even the big guy who'd blustered through their class, swearing that jumping out of a plane would be as fun as jumping into bed, had turned a chalky shade of green. He'd claimed it was only girls who had second thoughts, but now that it was crunch time he was looking anything but sure of himself.

One of the tandem jumpers leaned forward and yelled to the other positioned at the front, near the open door. "What's the holdup?"

The man mimed, "Dunno."

The pilot adjusted his headphones and turned to look over his shoulder. "Waiting for someone!"

Julia unclenched her hands and placed them on her knees. As long as it wasn't mechanical failure, she could handle a delay. It gave her time to think, something she clearly hadn't been doing too much of lately. Now that the plane was about to take off, she couldn't imagine why she'd believed skydiving was a good idea. There had to be a reason behind her impulse, but all that had flown out of her mind now that there was no turning back.

The other female student was nervously asking if there were barf bags aboard the airplane. Her tandem partner winced behind her back.

Sheesh. Julia was glad she'd had the foresight to decline breakfast. She moved restlessly on her floor cushion, tugging at the collar of her jumpsuit because she was sure it was choking her. Her brain was zipping from thought to thought, doing one-eighties every ten seconds. They'd better get going before she changed her mind and bolted for the open hatch.

She leaned forward, squinting across the airstrip at the simple wooden building and large old barn that housed the skydiving school. She'd chosen Sky Dancers off the Internet because she liked the name and because she'd never been to California before. At the time, booking the last-minute trip had seemed like a spontaneous, free-spirited impulse. The old Julia, the play-it-safe one, would have thoroughly checked all safety records and Better Business Bureau complaints, compared prices and studied up on the legalese in the liability releases. The new Julia had grabbed the whim and run with it no more than an hour after Adam had told her he was leaving.

That was another idea of hers that had seemed like a smart move at the time. Being the first to go instead of the one who stayed behind.

Once she'd arrived in California and checked into a modest hotel in the small desert town nearest to the airstrip, the momentum of this crazy idea had built, and she'd carried on regardless of her plentiful second thoughts. Yesterday she'd gone through the tandem-jump class, practiced the exit from the plane and the landing techniques where her job was mainly to stay out of the way of her partner. The tandem sky dive had been put off when the wind had picked up late yesterday afternoon, making the conditions too risky for beginners.

But today the weather was excellent.

And, by golly, she was going to jump out of an airplane.

Julia's stomach did a pitch-and-roll maneuver worthy of any stunt pilot. She swallowed and ducked forward, intending to put her head between her knees. That was when she saw the latecomer running across the tarmac toward the plane. It was a man, anonymous in the school's helmet and Kermit-green jumpsuit, but the way he moved reminded her of Adam. She closed her eyes. Put her forehead on her knees. Zack had told her that she didn't need to prove herself to Adam, but he'd misunderstood. She was doing this for herself. No one but herself.

Two of the jump instructors had risen and were talking to the newcomer, discussing his unscheduled arrival in loud voices. Julia caught a few words of the conversation—something about a replacement—and lifted her head to listen more closely. One of the jumpsuited figures stepped out of the airplane and closed the door behind himself. Word was sent forward to the pilot. The others shifted around, jostling as they took their places on the floor. The airplane taxied into position for take-off.

Julia's green-suited tandem partner came to sit beside her. She nudged him. "What's going on?"

He turned to look at her, saying something she didn't hear because she was too stunned by the familiarity of the eyes staring into hers. "*Adam?*" she said, her voice so weak all he would know was that she was moving her lips. "It can't be...."

He put his mouth near her ear. "I'm jumping with you!"

The plane was racing along the runway, engines whining, but the loudest roar of all was going on inside her head. She grabbed him by the arm and yelled, "What are you doing here?"

"Jumping," he said again. "With you!"

"But—but how?"

The plane lifted off the runway. Adam had his arm around her, and she was grateful for his presence even though it was causing her head and her stomach to swirl in crazy, opposing patterns. "How?" she hollered again as the airplane soared up into the sky.

"I used to live in California. I'm certified." He kissed her. "It'll be okay. Trust me."

Questions and confusion continued to spiral through her like a tangled parachute twisting in the wind. Yesterday, she'd seen a videotape of possible disasters and had managed to comfort herself with the knowledge that statistically, she was safer jumping out of a plane than traveling the LA freeways. But having Adam with her—even unexpectedly—was a far better comfort. She put her arm around his waist, leaning into him for a moment, drawing strength from his presence. He was all that she needed. "I've always trusted you," she said in a normal voice, sure he couldn't hear when her cheek pressed to his chest, "nearly as much as I've loved you."

Adam cupped her face, turning it to his own. "I know that. I finally figured it out—all of it."

All of what? she wanted to ask, but an intimate conversation was impossible when every word had to be shouted. She contented herself with lacing her fingers through his, bumping shoulders companionably as they climbed higher and higher into the sky.

The students had been told that reaching their jump altitude of ten thousand feet would take about twenty minutes. The time passed faster than Julia had expected. The main instructor, a strawberry blonde named Amy, stood and went through the procedure for exiting the plane one last time. Then she opened the door to a patch of endless blue sky.

Julia's eyes narrowed at the shrieking wind. The sound of the engines changed as the pilot throttled down, slowing their speed as they approached the target area. The others began maneuvering in the stripped-down airplane, the tandem-jump partners fastening the hooks that attached their harnesses to the students', the instructor going from student to student, checking the gear and soothing last-minute jitters. They'd rehearsed every move, so the preparations seemed strangely familiar. It was an awkward but beautiful ballet, first happening too fast for Julia to take in, and several seconds later seeming dreamily slow.

"C'mon. Let's get going." Adam helped her to her feet. Before he buckled them together, he put his mouth against her ear to ask again. "You're sure? You don't have to do this. It's not a requirement for loving me."

She shivered. Even amid the roar and bustle and fear, his warm breath and caring words gave her a ticklish thrill. In part of her mind, the option of backing out was an attractive one, but when she opened her mouth the opposite came out. "I want to! I really do!"

And she did.

She and Adam were going to fly.

He stepped behind her and attached their harnesses, tugging on every fastening before giving Julia a thumbs-up. Amy came over to ascertain that her student was okay with the last-minute change of partners, though it was clear to everyone aboard that Julia and Adam were already acquainted.

Julia pulled her goggles over her eyes as they got into position behind the other two teams. Even though Adam's arrival had shocked her, she was thrilled to have him behind her instead of a stranger. The procedure was the same, but the intimacy level had escalated, making the sky dive more than an experience.

It was a life-changing event.

Nevertheless, a panicky thought hit her as the first tandem pair stepped out the open door onto the strut and then suddenly disappeared, plummeting toward earth. She clutched for Adam's hands. If neither of his chutes opened, they'd *both* be goners. That seemed immeasurably worse than a solo tragedy. For a silent screaming instant, she couldn't bear the responsibility of knowing that her quest for change had come down to her risking Adam's life in addition to her own.

But he was right there with her, attuned to her emotions. He pulled his hands free so he could put his arms around her from behind, hugging her tight. "Don't worry. *We can do it.*"

No use yelling. She nodded, swallowing the lump that had risen in her throat as the second tandem jumpers exited the airplane. "Are *you* sure?"

"A thousand percent."

She crossed her arms over her chest as they shuffled toward the door. The opening yawned before her; instinctive fear made her cringe as she placed her feet on the strut. For a moment she focused only on the clear blue sky stretched out before her without end, but then she risked a glance at the earth, too far below for her to absorb the distance. Her stomach swooped.

This is crazy, it's nuts, it's the wildest idea I ever had and I'll pay a million dollars if only I could be back in Quimby right now with my feet planted safely on the ground—

"Ready?" Adam said, swinging onto the strut. She lifted her feet, letting them dangle as she'd been instructed. She was supported only by the harness.

And Adam.

"Ready," she shouted. *Please, God, keep us safe.*

They leaped.

10

IT WAS LIKE FLYING.

Rationally, Julia knew her body was on the bed, entwined with Adam's, but that didn't seem to matter. She'd transcended the merely physical. She was soaring.

Adam, too. He was right there with her, gliding beyond the glorious, soul-shattering release and into the heavens. They clutched hands, staring into each other's eyes. They smiled.

This will last forever, Julia thought.

We're never coming down....

THE GROUND was hard and warm and unmoving beneath her. Absolutely, positively the best sensation in the world. Lovely, lovely ground. She'd kiss it if it wasn't so...well, dirty.

Adam's face moved into her field of vision, blotting out the bright orb of the sun as he dropped a kiss onto her lips. She reached up with a lazy hand to stroke his stubbly cheek, drawing him down to her parted lips for a second kiss. Soft lips, warm mouth, velvet tongue, the honeyed tang of kisses that ran in a glittering river all the way to her toes.

Okay, the ground was the *second-best* sensation in the world.

She curled into him, pressing more kisses along his jawbone, down to his collar. "I'm telling you right now," she said with a soft laugh, "I'm never doing that again." At one time, she might have worried that her cowardice would bother him, but no more. Adam wasn't like that.

He slipped an arm beneath her, cushioning her from the hard-packed desert ground where she'd gratefully collapsed after meandering out of Sky Dancers with a goofy look on her face, too strung out by the emotions coursing through her to stay upright any longer. She'd felt exhilarated by the experience, amazed that all her limbs and organs were intact, then exhausted in the crashing aftermath of the pure adrenaline rush.

"Never again?" Adam murmured. "I hope you don't mean kissing me."

She chuckled. "Oh, no. *That's* something I plan to do every day for the rest of my life." As soon as the words were out, she regretted them. Oh, boy. Now he'd think she was proposing.

He surprised her by leaning closer to whisper, "Is that a promise?" in her ear.

"For as long as we're together," she said, playing it more cautiously this time.

"That reminds me of a skydiving joke. Typical gallows humor. Should I tell it?"

"Mm. Now that I've survived, I can probably even laugh at it."

Adam looped his other arm around her and pulled her partway into his lap. "The nervous beginner asks the instructor how long he has if his parachute doesn't open, and the instructor says..." He tilted his face toward hers, his eyes glinting. "The rest of your life."

Julia groaned. "Oh, ha, ha." She slid her hand from his chest to tweak his earlobe. "Thanks for not telling me that one up in the plane."

His lashes lowered as he scanned her face. "It seemed as though you enjoyed the jump."

"I did. I'm just never doing it again." She tilted her head against his chest to gaze at the cloudless sky. The sky dive had been incredible. Incredibly scary, too, but after a few seconds of sheer terror she'd found herself enjoying it. The free fall hadn't been the rapid, out-of-control, falling sensation she'd imagined. It had been more like floating, supported on a cushion of air even as the chilly high-altitude wind rushed over her body. Adam had been able to talk to her in brief snatches, and soon she'd relaxed enough to enjoy the magnificent panorama of sky and horizon, the mountains and flat brown earth of the valley, patchworked by fields and orange groves and buildings and roads.

There'd been a great jolt when Adam pulled the rip cord that released the parachute, and Julia's heart had given a wallop even though she'd been told to expect it. Then they were caught in the parachute's billowing, graceful descent, swinging in the harnesses, with Adam skillfully working the control lines so they glided slowly toward the ground. The landing had been a bit of an awkward tumble because of the ungainliness of the tandem harness. Julia hadn't minded. Her laughter had risen untethered and unabashed as he rolled beneath her, holding her securely in his arms. For a few seconds they were like a turtle upended onto its shell, limbs waggling uselessly in the air, and then he'd unbuckled the harness, and she'd slid free, regretting for an instant that they were separated before the elation struck her and she threw herself into his arms again, whooping with amazement that she'd done it and joy that she'd never, ever have to do it again.

"This was a once-in-a-lifetime experience for me,"

she said. "And believe me when I say I'm keeping it to *once.*"

"I don't know. You've got a hidden wild streak, woman. I was stunned when I figured out where you'd gone."

She smiled. Good. It didn't hurt to keep him guessing. "How did you track me down?"

"Simple. Your travel agent has a big mouth." He stroked her arms, gathering her against his chest. "But you left me a pretty good clue in your talk with Zack. What was that about?"

It was about getting you to come after me, you dope. "I'm not following."

"Why did you say you had to prove yourself? I've never suggested that to you, have I?"

"No, of course not." She got her feet under her and boosted herself to a sitting position, surprised by how weak-kneed she still felt. Adam might have to carry her to the car. "I did it to prove something to *myself.*"

"Which was?"

She laughed. "I thought it was simply that I could do it. But it turns out that it's more a case of never having to do it again, because now I know it's just not necessary. I might not be an adventurous risk-taker, but I don't have to be, either."

"I could have told you that."

"I liked the rock-climbing lessons, though. I might keep at it after I go back to Quimby."

"That's good," Adam said absently, his mind obviously on the skydiving, which she couldn't explain any more than she could a trip to the moon. "But why California?"

"What is it you said to me once? Because it's there?" She gave a half laugh. "Someday I'll be able to tell my grandchildren that I once took a whirlwind trip to California to go skydiving. Isn't that a good enough reason?"

"Grandchildren, huh?"

"Yup." She'd been careful to say *her* grandchildren, not *ours*. Where Adam Madman Brody was concerned, it wasn't safe to assume a thing.

"Then what's with the For Sale sign out front of your house? And the white-haired Julia Knox wanna-be who's taken over your office?"

Uh-oh. That kinda cut it.

"Well, uh, that's Kay Estress. She used to work for Cathy at her shop, until Cathy finally got rid of her. Kay decided to go into real estate. She's been working out of my office, so, you know, it was easiest to turn operations over to her."

"Right. And the house?"

Julia laughed nervously. "What is this, an interrogation?" She pulled away from him and pushed herself to her feet. Tentatively.

He leaped up and extended a hand. "Take it easy. You're an adrenaline virgin."

She shot him a wry grin. "Not a virgin. An amateur, perhaps."

He steadied her as they walked toward the parking area. "Whew," she said. "That was quite a rush. At least now I'll understand a little better what you're feeling when you're out there with your new team, risking life and limb in all four corners of the globe." Her voice rang out bright and chipper in the desert air. Maybe she'd laid it on a little too thick.

"The house?" Adam said. "Why are you selling your house, Julia? You love that house."

She leaned against her rental car, saying, "Oh,

damn," under her breath. She was going to have to come clean.

Deep breath. "A house is just a house. It doesn't mean anything without the people you love living there."

He cocked his head, smiling at her very faintly. "The people? Who are these people?"

She blinked. Oh, all right. She could say it. "The man. The man I love." Her heart was hammering as hard as it had when she'd stood at the open door of the airplane. "In other words, *you,* Adam. You mean more to me than a house."

His expression remained inscrutable. How frustrating. He was so contained that one day she'd have set a firecracker off beneath him just to see the look of surprise on his face.

"That doesn't explain why you're selling it."

"Can't you figure it out?"

He touched her, his fingers gently smoothing her tangled haystack of hair.

She gave in. "It's the same old story," she said. "If you weren't smart enough to ask me along—and so far, may I point out, you *weren't*—I was going to go to you. Because I'd rather be in Colorado with you than in Quimby all alone."

"Aw, Goldie." He put his arms around her waist, lifted her off her feet and swung her around. She gloried in the embrace. It was as big a thrill as a free fall from ten thousand feet. Better, even, because this was the kind of feeling that would last forever.

She slid along his body until her toes touched ground. They were both grinning like fools until Adam sobered.

"You have such a good life in Quimby," he persisted. "I can't ask you to leave that behind for the likes of me."

"Can't?" She tilted her chin at him. "Or is it that you just don't dare?"

His eyes narrowed. "Now, hold on. Before you get all superior on me, may I point out that this time I came to you? And it wasn't any trip around the corner. It was all the way to California. That should earn me a few brownie points."

She blinked. Sweet heaven on earth, he was right.

Adam Brody, the goodbye man, had come to her.

She shook her head in disbelief. "Well, I'll be damned. Does that mean what I hope it means?"

His arms tightened around her. "It means I love you."

"And?" she prompted, packing a thousand watts of happiness in her smile but determined to make him work to reach the On switch.

"It means that I'd be honored if you'd be crazy enough to come along with me to Colorado."

She tossed her hair. "Oh, I'm crazy enough, all right. Today has to be good for proving that, at least."

"And it means..." Adam's voice dropped, infused with all the emotion that didn't show on his face. "It means that even though I'm not likely to ever be a normal type of beer-in-the-BarcaLounger sort of a husband, I'd like to take a shot at it anyway. I'd like to marry you, Julia."

Her beaming brilliance could have outshone the sun. "You goof. I don't want a beer-in-the-Barca Lounger husband. I want *you*."

He laughed. "You *are* crazy."

"Yes, sirree. Crazy in love."

"Do I get to kiss you now?"

"Just one thing." She dug a hand into the pocket of her jeans and pulled out the small red granite pebble. "This isn't a valuable gemstone or a longtime treasure. But it means something special to me—it represents the day I took a chance and changed my life. Will you take it...this time?"

"Yes. Thank you." Adam lifted it from her fingers, and she knew that he was accepting more than a token rock. He was opening his heart to her love, acknowledging his human frailty and hers at the same time he acknowledged that their union made them stronger than either one of them could ever be alone.

"And this is for you," he said softly, suddenly producing the smooth gray stone he'd shown her in the cupola.

She opened her palm, and he dropped the stone into it. "But I thought this was lost."

"I went back and found it."

"Are you sure you want to give it to me?"

"I don't need it now that I have you."

"Oh, Adam." She folded her fingers around the stone and threw her arms around his neck. "You know what? Now would be a really good time to kiss me."

Which he did until she broke away, half gasping, half laughing. She gazed at him for a moment, then wonderingly touched a fingertip to his lips. "There will be people back in Quimby who'll call our marriage a very risky proposition. Just how long do you think we have?"

In the span of a few minutes, Adam's face had transformed. She was transfixed to see his love for her evident in his quick frown, in his even quicker smile, and especially in the soft green glow of eyes. "That's an easy answer. We have the rest of our lives, Goldie. *The rest of our lives.*"